Sword
of
Phoenix

Sword of Phoenix

By

Ronald E. Whitley

Order this book online at www.trafford.com
or email orders@trafford.com

Most Trafford titles are also available at major online book retailers.

Printed in the United States of America.

ISBN: 978-1-4269-5236-4 (sc)
ISBN: 978-1-4269-5237-1 (e)

Library of Congress Control Number: 2010918814

Trafford rev. 12/15/2010

 www.trafford.com

North America & International
toll-free: 1 888 232 4444 (USA & Canada)
phone: 250 383 6864 ✦ fax: 812 355 4082

INTRODUCTION

In Vietnam, the Central Intelligence Agency (CIA), in conjunction with MACV SOG, Military Assistance Command, Vietnam, Studies and Observation Group (A joint service command consisting of elements the United States Army, the Marine Corps, the Air Force, and Special Forces units from 5th Special Forces Group and Navy Seal Teams) were authorized, by Command Authority at the Pentagon, to conduct covert operations and missions within and outside the borders of South Vietnam, including Laos, Cambodia and North Vietnam.

Mission Statement: "to execute an intensified program of harassment, diversion, political pressure, capture of prisoners, physical destruction, acquisition of intelligence, generation of propaganda, and diversion of resources, against North Vietnam and the National

Front for the Liberation of South Vietnam (NLF or derogatively, Viet Cong) insurgency."

Several agencies were used to funnel money and material to these operations. One of these was VE-AD, the Vietnamese Economic Agricultural Development Agency.

One of the operations conducted was Phoenix. The Phoenix Program was a military, intelligence, and internal security program designed by the CIA and coordinated with the Republic of Vietnam's security apparatus during the Vietnam War. It was in operation between 1967 and 1972, but similar efforts existed both before and after this. The program was designed to identify and "neutralize" (via infiltration, capture, or assassination) the civilian infrastructure supporting the Viet Cong insurgency.

Sword of Phoenix is a true story, although parts are fictionalized to facilitate the telling of the story. Most characters are based on real people and some are based on composites of different people. With few exceptions, names have been changed and in some cases the time line and locations. This is not meant to be a historical or chronological record of events. The Phoenix Program has been described by Presidents and Generals as being an operation to win the hearts and minds of the Vietnamese people. I am not here to contradict these men as they were at the top of the totem pole and I was at the bottom, where the rubber meets the road. I can only tell the story from the point of view which I was involved. Although Operation Phoenix is only a small part of this book, it is an important part. There is no intent by the me to discredit or malign any person or group of persons depicted in this book.

Sword of Phoenix is dedicated to all of America's warriors who have fallen in harms way, whether they served in uniform or in the shadows. Their names may fade, and their deeds may be lost in history, but they will live forever in every child born in freedom.

SWORD OF PHOENIX

An original novel by:

Ronald E. Whitley

Read also:

Code Name: Viking, by Ronald E. Whitley, Trafford Publishing\07-1397. ISBN 1-4251-3577-3

The Pacific Hotel, by Ronald E. Whitley, Trafford Publishing\06-1217 ISBN 1-4120-9462-3 Available at trafford.com

Author welcomes questions and comments and may be contacted at PO Box 424, Brandenburg, KY, USA, 40108

CHAPTER 1

Vietnam, The "F N G"

Well, here I am, from beautiful clean Germany to not so clean Vietnam, the foulest smelling place I have ever been in my 20 years of life. I guess I should tell you who I am, so here goes. The name is Whitley, I'm a brand new Staff Sergeant, been in the Army a little over three years now, and have had a very strange and unusual career so far, but now there is no doubt, I'm *In the Army Now*, right in the middle of a war.

In Germany, I had been selected, or more apt compelled into a job that was not in your normal *Line of Duty*, and got into some serious problems, through no fault of my own. The Operation I was on ended badly, very badly, and I was shuffled back into the deck with some bad memories that I was trying very hard to put behind me. *Murphy's Law* says that, *"Anything that can go wrong, will go wrong."* and it could not have applied more to Operation Norseman. Then there is the *Peter Principal* that says, *"People are promoted to their level of incompetence"* or, *"screw up, move up."* . As I said, here I am, a brand new Staff Sergeant.

I was assigned to Vietnam as an Intelligence Area Analysts, now don't ask me what that is, because I haven't been to the school yet. I was scheduled to go when I was assigned to Vietnam because of a critical shortage in that MOS (Military Occupational Specialty), yet another example of *Murphy's Law.*

I had spent one miserable night in the reception area, the heat, humidity and foul odor that emanates from this place is unbelievable. The next morning my name was called over the loud speaker and I was picked up by two MI (Military Intelligence) Agents. One of them was in uniform, but I had no idea what rank he was, because he was only wearing U.S. collar pins and no insignia of rank. The other was wearing a bright red, yellow and green Aloha shirt, which I was to find out was the preferred uniform for a lot of the MI and CID Agents that worked in the rear areas, short of being assigned to a Headquarters.

The one in uniform told me that I was going to be assigned to the field unit attached to the 9th Infantry Division, but he didn't know what my job would be. Then he said he had orders to take me by the Embassy first. When I asked him what for, he just said. "Orders, that's all, just orders. You *do* know what those are. Don't you Sergeant?" The one in the Aloha shirt laughed and said. "Don't worry, you're going to love Vietnam."

At the Embassy, I was taken to a small office, out of the way from the main flow of things around the other busy offices and told to go on in and they will wait for me.

The next thing that that happened was not only unexpected, but a nightmare for me.

"Welcome to Vietnam, Viking." The man behind the desk said. It was Jack Roark and I was speechless.

Viking had been my code name on Operation Norseman and Jack Roark was the son-of-a-bitch that got me involved in that mess and the very last person that I ever wanted to see again. Roark was supposed to be a Cultural Attaché with the Embassy, but I knew that was just a bullshit cover for what ever his real job was.

"I didn't expect to see you again." That was all I could summon to say. It may have sounded dumb but I was still in shock.

"Hell Whitley, don't take it so big. We Kentucky boys have to look out for each other. Anyway, I wanted to make sure you got that promotion. Those Staff Sergeant stripes look good on you."

"Yeah, I wondered if that mess in France had anything to do with the promotion."

"Look Whitley. Just because the Operation went south doesn't mean it was your fault. From what I understand, you did good, handled yourself exceptionally well for a bad situation, and most importantly, kept your mouth shut. Anyway, I wanted you to know where I am located, I might have a job or two for you while you are here." He said while looking away and fiddling with something on his desk.

"And I suppose I have you to thank for being here in Vietnam." I said accusingly.

"No, that was all the Army, just the luck of the draw, I guess." He said as he looked up from the papers he was messing with, and I am not sure I believed him.

"Well how did you know I was on my way, if you didn't have anything to do with it?"

"Look son, you're an asset and we keep track of our assets, and its part of my job to know what assets are available in my area." He said as he stood up and offered no further explanation, then continued. "I understand you are going to the 9th Infantry Division at Bear Cat. You'll like the Detachment Commander, he's not a Kentucky boy, but close enough, he's from West Virginia and he went to school at UofK, and like I said you'll like him, he is what you would call a friend of ours."

"A friend of ours?" I asked, but he ignored the question.

"Well Whitley, stay safe out there, and you may be hearing from me." He said as he extended his arm to shake hands. I guess it was his way of telling me the meeting was over.

"Yeah, you too, Mister Roark." I did shake his hand out of common courtesy, although it was without regard, as I really don't like this man.

I left the embassy with the two guys that had picked me up from the replacement depot, and after a short ride we pulled up to what looked like a private compound located in the city. The driveway was closed off by large solid metal gates that were opened by two armed Vietnamese guards in civilian clothes. There was rolled barbed wire on top of the gates as well as on top of the twelve-foot wall surrounding the compound. The chipped painted sign on the left hand gate read "Vietnamese Economic Agricultural Development Agency", the sign on the right hand gate, I assume, said the same thing in Vietnamese.

On our way to an office inside the main building, I saw inside a large map room while a man in civilian clothes was exiting. The door was quickly closed behind him, but it was open long enough for me to see what looked like a TOC (Tactical Operations Center). Most of the people inside were in civilian clothes, but there was a small hand full in military uniforms, both US Army and Vietnamese Army Officers.

My escort in the Aloha shirt left us and the one in the jungle fatigues took me on down the hall and knocked on a door, the sign outside just read, "G. A. Augden, VE-AD Coordinator". After a response from inside the office, we entered, and my escort said to the man behind the desk, "I've got the F.N.G., Boss.", as he placed the large manila envelope he was carrying on it.

"Thanks, Pete. Lt. Parrish will take it from here. Wait a second Pete, let me have one of those Kools of yours." Said Augden, the man behind the desk as he pulled my 201 file out of the envelope.

"I thought you quit smoking Boss." Pete said as he pulled a plastic cigarette case out of his pocket, opened it and offered one to him.

"Oh well, crap changes from day to day around here, you know that." Augden said as he took one and lit it, with that Pete left the office.

"Have a seat, Sergeant Whitley." Augden read my 201 file for a moment then said. "I understand you have never worked as an analyst." "Is that correct?"

"Yes Sir, that's correct, I was assigned in my secondary MOS. I was scheduled to go to the school when I got back to the States, but I got orders for Vietnam instead."

"Is that going to be a problem, Parrish?" Augden addressed the other man in the room.

"No Sir, not on the Contact Team, we'll teach him what he needs to know." Parrish replied.

"OK then. Sergeant Whitley, this is Lt. Parrish, he is the number two man at the detachment you are being assigned. He will take care of you from here, and Whitley, when he tells you something, bet on it. It's not the free ride over here, that everyone back in Washington thinks it is." Augden said as he put my 201 file back into the envelope and slid it across the desk toward Lt. Parrish.

"Yes Sir." I replied and stood up as Lt. Parrish did. I waited to see if Parrish saluted Augden, he did not, so I didn't either, we just left the office.

Parrish was young, not much older than I am. He was dressed in jungle fatigues with a 45 auto in an army style shoulder holster. He was not wearing lieutenant bars, so I didn't know if he was a First or Second Lieutenant, just the same US collar pins that Pete had been wearing. When we got to the jeep, he retrieved his M16 rifle from one of the guards and handed it to me. This was the first time I had seen an M16 up close, we were still using the M14 rifle in Germany. I was amazed as to how light it was, it felt like a toy compared to the M14 I had been lugging around in the field in Germany. We left the compound and drove through the streets to another compound, the main APO (army post office). I don't mind telling you, I was a little unnerved, the streets of Saigon are more than just crowded, there are people everywhere, on motor scooters, cyclos, bicycles, taxi's, cars, trucks, push carts loaded with produce, and military vehicles, all mixed together going in every direction. I thought driving in Paris or Rome was bad, but this is utter chaos.

At the APO we had lunch in the mess hall and waited for the afternoon mail trucks going to Camp Bear Cat and joined the two mail trucks and escort vehicle, a ¾-ton truck mounted with a M60 machine gun in the bed. In convoy we headed out to join the traffic. It was about an hour and a half drive and I was soaking wet with sweat by the time we arrived at Bear Cat. We followed one of the mail trucks through the main gate, the second mail truck and escort vehicle continued on to somewhere else. Once on post we headed to the detachment headquarters.

When we arrived and started toward the door, I heard someone inside yell out, "Hey Captain, the L. T. is back with the F.N.G.."

"That's Caffey, I think he's been here too long, but you'll get use to him." Parrish said as we entered the building. "Caffey this is Sergeant Whitley, Whitley meet Specialist Five Caffey, he's the combination detachment clerk, supply sergeant, maker of the coffee, keeper of the fridge, and all around gopher."

"Caffey." I said.

"What, what, did I hear something, I'm so short I think it is affecting my hearing. Just kidding Sarg, you'll love it here, if you live long enough."

"Caffey, the mail truck is in, why don't you go do something useful." Parrish said.

"But L. T., I was just about to type up my request for a 6 month extension here. Just kidding L. T., your wish is my command." Caffey said then got up from his desk and left the building.

"Just ignore his smart ass mouth, Caffey is a good man and can get you just about anything you need around here, and spent 6 months on a Contact Team before being shot in the ass, by accident, by the MP on his team. At least the MP said it was an accident. Anyway, you'll get use to him."

"Parrish, you out there?" Came the voice from the Commander's office.

"Yes Sir, be right there. Come on and meet Captain Sullivan." Parrish said as he knocked on the Detachment Commander's door and we went in.

I reported to Captain Sullivan, and he returned my salute and told me to have a seat. He spent a couple of minutes going over my 201 file then finally started to speak. "We are part of the 525th Military Intelligence Group assigned to MACV (Military Assistance Command, Vietnam) and attached to the 584th Military Intelligence Company which is part of the 9th Infantry Division, they do mostly PSYOPS (psychological warfare) and Counter Intelligence, but we are a separate entity, and anything that we do, does not concern them. What I am saying is, when dealing with the Company be respectful and maintain military decorum, but what goes on here, stays here. Understand?"

"Yes Sir, but what is it that we do here?"

"We coordinate the logistics for covert operations in our area, but that is mostly handled here in the office by Bill Morgan, or "Big M", as he is referred to, Caffey and Lt. Parrish. You met Caffey, I suppose. We also run three POW Contact Teams that is what you are going to be doing. Each team consist of a team leader, that's you, you'll be replacing Lt. Mike Parr, and you'll have a MP, and a Vietnamese MI Agent who also serves as the translator, on your team his name is Nyguen Tran Puk, Tran for short. Papa Tango 2 should be in sometime tomorrow and you will be able to meet Parr and Tran.

We have six MPs assigned to the detachment, including SFC Williams, and they rotate with the teams, so when you go out, you'll get whoever is on the top of the list. They also provide POW transport to Saigon. Questions so far?"

"Yes Sir, what does a POW Contact Team do?"

"When line units capture POWs, a team goes out to evaluate the prisoners. If North Vietnamese political cadre or NVA regulars, you bring them back here for shipment to Saigon for the Pro's at the 525th to process. If Viet Cong of intelligence value, rely on Tran for that, they come back here for shipment to Saigon, if considered to be of no intelligence value, they are released to the military commander there, and they will probably be turned over to the ARVN (Army, Republic of Vietnam) Commander. There, they most likely are executed but that is not our business, I mean it's their war. The third type could be innocent civilians picked up in a sweep, again, rely on Tran's advice to make that determination. If that is the case, you release them to the military commander with a recommendation that they be let go. Remember, you are only making a recommendation, what happens to them from that point is not our business. Understand so far?"

"So far, Sir."

"Papa Tango 2 works mainly II Corps, as you can see on the map, you'll have a big area that encompasses a lot of different units, Army and Marines. There are three other teams out there, Papa Alpha teams, each stationed in, and assigned to a specific Corps area, so we are backup, but don't let that fool you, you'll be in the bush more than you are here. There will be times that you may get some flak from the unit S2s (staff intelligence officers), so you will have to lose those stripes. It is better if they don't know what rank you are, it is just easier if they don't know whether they out-rank you or not." Captain Sullivan paused for a moment while he reached into his desk drawer for a pair of subdued US collar pins and tossed them to me. Then continued. "Look, Whitley, you'll do fine. Go with Lt. Parr and Tran on their next run, then you take over. In the mean time Lt. Parrish will fill you in on details and get you situated with the Company." With that Parrish stood up so I did too, but then Sullivan continued. "Lt. Parrish, will you excuse us for a moment."

"Yes Sir, I'll be in the outer office." Lt. Parrish left the room and closed the door.

"I don't know what your relationship is to Roark, and don't want to know, but while you are here you work for me. You don't take orders from Roark, you take orders from me. Am I making myself clear Sergeant?"

"Yes Sir, very much so."

"OK, that will be all."

With that I saluted and left the office. Well the Captain didn't have to worry about me, Jack Roark is the last son-of-a-bitch in the world that I want anything to do with. Lt. Parrish and I walked over to the Company, it was only a couple of buildings behind our office. While there, I got a room assignment and drew field gear including a 45 cal. Pistol and a M16, flak jacket, and steel pot. I asked a lot of questions while we walked back to the office, got into one of the two jeeps in front, then went on a brief tour of the post to show me where the PX, clubs, and swimming pool were located. I learned that Colonel Augden was the big boss, but we didn't work for VE-AD. Colonel Augden, like a lot of the commanders, wore two hats. Therefore, our association with the Vietnamese Economic, Agricultural Development Agency was only through Colonel Augden.

Parrish told me that Tran was one of the best and I was lucky to be working with him and that Lt. Parr, the guy I was replacing had spent almost his whole tour in the bush, first with one of the Papa Alpha teams then with us on a Papa Tango team. Parr was rotating out in three more weeks. Bill Morgan, on the other hand was a Chief Warrant Officer and *an old school spook* (a spook is what Intelligence Agents are called that are involved in active fieldwork), was starting his third tour in Vietnam. When I asked Parrish if "Big M" was his code name, he laughed and said no, it was one of his nicknames. The girls at the local boom boom parlor call him, "Little Willy", and "Little organ", so we all call him, "Big M" (little organ) for Morgan. I had to laugh too, it was funny and I wondered if Morgan knew what "Big M" really stood for. When I asked him what F.N.G. stood for, he looked over at me, and just said, *"Fuckin' New Guy."* "That's you."

CHAPTER 2

Papa Tango Two

I spent the next two days trying to get acclimated to this heat. Waking up to the smell of burning crap and diesel fuel as they dispose of the latrine waste from the day before. The smell doesn't go away, you just get use to it after a day or two, and it is still hot, but I guess you just don't notice it as much the longer you have been here. The guys around the Company didn't talk to us much because we weren't *real soldiers,* being assigned to MACV support. Since they don't know what we do, they just assume we don't do anything, including pulling any duties like Staff Duty Officer or Guard duty and that was fine with me, and exactly the way Captain Sullivan wanted it. Like he said, what we do is none of their business.

I was eating morning chow in the mess hall, when Caffey came in and sat across from me, and said in a low voice, "Parr and Tran are back and they have a Viet Cong Political officer with them, if you want to get a look at what you will be going after." Then started eating his breakfast.

"Yeah, I will, thanks Caffey." I said as I finished eating. As I got up and started to leave, Caffey asked me to get a bowl of rice and gravy and take it to the prisoner.

I got the rice, they were out of gravy, so I put some bacon on top of the rice and headed to the office. When I got there, one of the MPs was sitting at Caffey's desk and beside him, on the floor, was the prisoner. A Vietnamese in uniform, that looked like he weighs a hundred pounds including the leg shackles and handcuffs he was wearing. I sat the bowl of rice on the corner of the desk and the MP looked at it then picked it up and showed it to the Charlie who nodded and said something in Vietnamese. The MP handed me his shotgun while he uncuffed one of Charlie's hands and hooked his other one to the leg shackles then handed him the bowl. Charlie nodded with his head several time and said what I guess was Vietnamese for thank you, over and over. The prisoner put the bowl in the hand that was still shackled and started eating with his fingers.

Captain Sullivan's door opened and I heard the Captain's voice. "Come in here Whitley, I want you to meet Lt. Parr."

"Yes Sir." I said and handed the MP his shotgun back and walked past the Vietnamcsc man in Tiger fatigues, who was holding the door open.

"Sergeant Whitley, this is Lt. Parr, and Parr this is your replacement."

"Glad to see you Sergeant, real glad. Just don't let anything happen to you till I get the hell out of this place." Parr smiled as we shuck hands.

"Good to meet you sir." I said as the Captain introduced Nyguen Tran Puk. "You too Sir, pleased to meet you. I understand we'll be working together."

"Tran, just call me Tran." He said in perfect English with only a hint of a French accent, and we also shuck hands. "Sergeant Whitley, I will be back in five days, we will get to know each other then. Captain, with your permission?"

"OK Tran, take off. See you in five days." Captain Sullivan said and Tran nodded in Lt. Parr's direction and left the room closing the door behind him. The Captain then continued. "Tran is going to take Sergeant William's place escorting the prisoner to Saigon and has some personal business to take care of and wants to spend some time with his family during TET (Vietnamese New Year), so Mike you might as well take a day or two off as well, then hook up with Whitley before your next assignment."

"That's what I was waiting to hear. Whitley, glad to meet you and like I said, don't you dare get shot or break a leg or something stupid like that, at least not for three more weeks". With that, Parr took his leave.

"Whitley, you hold down the office. Caffey is going with me and Lt. Parrish to a meeting at Division Operations and if Big M comes in, tell him to call a Commander Selcroft about those boats he wanted."

We both left his office and Tran and the MP guard were just pulling out with the prisoner,

"Caffey, let's go and give the keys to Lt. Parrish, there's no way you are driving."

"But Captain, I was just kidding about that suicide shit."

"Caffey, if you don't stop fuckin' around, I'm going to wait till you are down to two days then have you're ass committed to the nut ward just to keep you here. Now let's go."

"Yes Sir, Captain. No problem here." Caffey jumped up, clicked his heels like a Nazi soldier and saluted Sullivan.

About lunch time Bill Morgan came in to the office and wanted to know where everyone was. I told him that the Captain, Parrish and Caffey went to a meeting at Division Operations and gave him the message about Commander Selcroft.

"Great. I know what he wants. Can you type?" Big M asked as he was fumbling around in his brief case.

"Yes Sir."

"OK, here is a copy of a joint service equipment and manpower requirement. I need one just like this, only use this information." He said as he handed me another piece of paper. He then disappeared into his office after getting a cup of coffee.

It was simple enough, something called Operation Forester and was addressed to Commander Selcroft at River Flotilla One. It didn't have a whole lot of information on it except for two PBRs, River Patrol Boats, and crews. Mission statement: Classified. Destination: Classified. Duration of operation: Classified. Like I said, not a whole lot of information. When it got to the part for the Finance Accounting and Authorization Code, I knocked on Big M's door and asked him. He told me to use the MACV accounting number for everything unless told specifically to use the VE-AD number and I could find them in Caffey's top desk drawer.

Later on that afternoon Sergeant First Class Franks, Papa Tango Three, and his translator Mister Quan, reported in from their last job. I talked with Quan about what was going on up in the Parrot's Beak, that's the area they've just returned from. He told me that several units have engaged NVA (North Vietnamese Army) regulars along the Cambodian border. He said it was a pretty bad situation for the 9th Infantry Division's 3d Brigade, every time they hit the NVA and had them where they wanted, they would be hit from behind by Viet Cong. SFC Franks filled out his after action report and dropped it in Caffey's in-box. There were three prisoners, all Viet Cong soldiers, so they weren't brought back. While they were still in the office, Caffey and the Captain returned.

I started to head out because the office was getting crowded when the Captain spoke up.

"Sergeant Whitley, Caffey is going to be tied up with me for a couple of days. Since you won't be going out until Parr and Tran get back, I would like for to stick close to the office and help Big M and Parrish out as much as possible. That way you will gain a little insight into the other part of our job around here."

"No problem Sir. I'm just going to grab something to eat."

A couple of days later the night was particularly hot and I was having a hard time sleeping because of the humidity, so I decided to go take a shower and cool down. A chancy proposition around here since we don't have hot water heaters. Our showers are big tanks of water that are heated by the sun during the day. So much so, that the water is too hot to take a shower during the day, and usually cold by the next morning. Seven to eight pm seems to be the optimal time for a hot but not scalding shower. Three thirty in the morning you're taking a chance because the water may be warm or it may be cold, but what ever it is, I have got to do something to get more comfortable. I stopped outside the hooch and sat on the sand bags to smoke a cigarette before walking to the shower, which is located on the other side of the Company Headquarters building. I was just finishing my smoke when I heard three or four booms and the sirens starting going off, so I headed to the nearest bunker. Just as I reached the bunker, B40 rockets started coming in, and they were close, it sounded like one of them hit in the Company area and another not more than two buildings away. After the rockets, I could hear mortars being walked-in, but they were closer to the perimeter, a half mile or so away. I decided to head back to the hooch to get dressed, along with some of the other guys that were in the bunker by this time.

While getting dressed, more rockets were coming in, and the mortars were getting closer. Someone came running through the building yelling, "Get your weapons and report to the motor pool, the perimeter is being hit!"

In case I hadn't understood it before, this was the defining moment when I realized that this was not your normal hit and run, where Charlie pops in a few mortar rounds then it is all over, we were actually under attack. I put a clip into my "45" and grabbed both the loaded magazines I had for my M16 and threw on my steel pot. Caffey stuck his head into my still open door and asked. "Are you ready? This is a big one."

"I'm ready, let's go." I said as we headed out toward the motor pool along with four other guys from our building. I had to take my steel pot off and carry it, it was bouncing all over my head. There was one truck pulling out as we arrived at the motor pool, but there was another one loading, so we jumped onto the back of that one.

About six more guys jumped onto the truck while the Supply Sergeant and another soldier started throwing boxes of M16 ammunition, hand grenades, grenades for the M79s, and illumination flairs into the back of the truck.

"Who's in charge here? Who's the ranking man." Asked the Company Commander as he approached the back of the truck. I didn't say anything because the only guy I knew on the truck was Caffey.

"I think Staff Sergeant Whitley is." Caffey said as he was looking around at the other guys in the truck.

"Are you Sergeant Whitley?" The Captain asked.

"Yes Sir."

"OK Whitley, you are going to the south perimeter. Charlie is trying to come through the wire. Find Lt. Freelander, the officer of the guard, get this ammo to him and fill in with your men wherever he needs you." The Captain said, then continued. "OK driver, take off."

It was a short ride, about 5 minutes. The closer we got, the more small arms fire we could hear in front of us and mortars and rockets going off behind us landing some where on post. There was a Lieutenant there when we pulled in. Whether it was Freelander or not, I don't know, but he was giving orders to unload the truck, so I reported to him.

"Have your men each get at least two grenades, two flairs, a bandoleer of M16 ammo, and a box of ammo for the machine gunners. Go straight down the path, that'll take you up behind guard post 21, that's where the M60 is, drop the machine gun ammo there then split your men into three groups and fill in at 21, 22 and 23. Got it?"

"Got it." I replied, then continued. OK guys, you heard the Lieutenant, grab the ammo and let's go."

There was continuous probes by the VC and fire fights up and down the perimeter until almost daylight. You could see the red tracer rounds from our machine guns going out to the wire and green tracers coming back, bouncing and ricocheting all over the place. Two VC got through the wire in front of post 22 and got a grenade into the guard post killing two soldiers and wounding three more, before being killed themselves. Post 21, where Caffey and I were, was hit several times by RPGs, all but one went into the sand bags in front and below us, and the other one went way over our heads. We only had one man wounded on guard post 21 and two wounded on post 23. At 0600 hours, we got word via the field phone to cease fire unless we had an identifiable target, because the Striker force was out side the wire in pursuit of Charlie. Just before daylight I could see the tracers form a AC47 Spooky, like a red rope of fire coming out of the sky laying death on anyone or anything that it touched. At 0700 hours our artillery had finally ceased and we were relieved by soldiers from one of the Division's Infantry Battalions. Before leaving, I was amazed at the number of dead enemy in the wire, and how close some of them actually got to us, it seemed like hundreds, some in uniforms but most in those black PJs they wear. There was scores of ladders mixed in with the wire covered with body parts that had been shredded by the Claymore mines. It was then I realized how lucky we were to still be here and to have had the small number of casualties we did. There were other post down the line that didn't have the luck we did, but most of the guard posts didn't have any causalities at all.

We were driven by truck back to the Company area, and found out our mess hall had been hit, as well as several of the Conex containers outside the supply room right next to the officer's hooch. The Company Headquarters was roped off because of a dud rocket sticking out of the ground right next to the orderly room. One of the Company officers told us to keep our weapons with us and directed us to the Signal Company mess hall to eat. At chow the rumor mill was working overtime, someone said that Hué City had been over run and there were no survivors. I never heard so many wild stories and figured we would get the real lowdown when we got to the office.

Caffey noticed my hand shaking while I was eating and asked me. "Were you scared? If you were, you didn't show it out on the perimeter."

"When the hell do you have time to be scared? I don't know, maybe." I replied.

"Me, now I was scared shitless, but I think you are one of those guys that it doesn't hit you, until it's all over." Caffey continued with his little pearls. "You never know how someone is going to act. Take Big M for instance, I don't think that guy even goes to the bunker any more."

"Yeah, maybe, I don't know. Hell, I don't even know if it is over, besides you looked like an old pro out there with that M79 grenade launcher."

Captain Sullivan told us that there had been a coordinated attack all over South Vietnam. Several buildings on post had been hit including our mess hall, and VC sappers had hit the fuel and ammo dumps. The

Embassy was still under attack in Saigon, and there were some battles still going on up country including Hué City, but the majority of it was over, or soon would be, with the exception of Hué City and Khe Sanh still being under siege.

The next two days went by with occasional perimeter probes, night time mortars and rockets, and me helping out with the normal office crap. Lt. Parrish went out on Operation Forester, what ever that was. All the guys were pretty tight lipped about operations, even around the office. Everything, and I mean everything was "need to know". I was starting to see a lot of paper work go through about something called the Phoenix program and it was the only paper work that had the VE-AD accounting numbers on it.

I made my first assignment with Parr and Tran, it was exciting for me as it was my first trip into the bush. All the prisoners, Tran determined were just farmers that were picked up on a village sweep. They may have been VC, but no weapons or anything else was found on them, so they were released back to the Army commander with a recommendation that they be fed, given medical treatment and let go. Whether they were or not, who knows, because we didn't hang around, Parr called in a helicopter and we headed back to Bear Cat.

The next assignment, I made without Lt. Parr. We flew into a Marine Fire Support Base to evaluate three prisoners. The VC were being "questioned", by a Vietnamese Sergeant holding their heads one at a time under water in a fire barrel, and when they weren't the one in the barrel, they were being kicked and spit on by another Vietnamese soldier. Although Marines were not taking part in the abuse, the whole thing was taking place in front of a Marine Sergeant who was just watching. I was approaching the Marine Sergeant to put a stop to what was going on, when Tran beat me to it. He started yelling in Vietnamese at the Sergeant doing the dunking. An argument ensued and Tran slapped the Sergeant. The Sergeant reached for his pistol, but Tran slapped him again and pushed him over the fire barrel knocking him to the ground and Tran drew his pistol and pointed it at the Sergeant's head while he was on the ground. The whole thing was interrupted by two officers that joined the fray, a Marine Lieutenant and a ARVN Captain.

"What the hell's going on here, Sergeant Franco?" The Lieutenant addressed the Sergeant who had been observing the incident.

"Nothing Sir. Not a thing, except these jokers took exception to the way Sergeant Vu was questioning the prisoners." Franco replied then spit on the ground in my direction.

"Who the hell are you people?" The Marine Lieutenant was addressing me.

"The Contact Team, here to evaluate the prisoners, and we found your Sergeant here, allowing these two to torture these men."

"Men? I don't see any men. All I see is some VC scum that got stuck on the bottom of my men's boots."

"That'll be enough Franco!" Said the Lieutenant then Tran started in on the ARVN Captain.

"Unacceptable, unacceptable, absolutely unacceptable." Tran said then reverted to Vietnamese continuing to criticize the ARVN Captain.

"KNOCK IT OFF." Yelled the Master Gunnery Sergeant approaching with a Marine Captain, who must be the Fire Base Commander.

"What's going on here Lieutenant?" Asked the Captain.

"Just a little misunderstanding, Skipper. These guys are here for the prisoners, that's all."

The ARVN Captain finally spoke up and said something to Tran then to the soldier on the ground. Tran holstered his pistol and the ARVN Sergeant picked himself up off the ground and did a reluctant bow in Tran's direction.

"If they're here for the prisoners, then let them have them, Lieutenant, and get this shit under control. Understand?"

"Aye, aye Skipper."

The Captain and the Master Gunny continued on to where ever they were headed before they were attracted by the commotion.

"You heard the Skipper. You want the prisoners, then take them and un-ass my AO."

Well now we had no choice but to take the prisoners, even though these VC are of no intelligence value, and would normally have been released back to the unit commander for his disposition. So my first mission as the team leader turns out to be a total screw up. I hope this isn't a sign of things to come, but I very seldom get what I hope for. Nothing left to do now, but to call the Triple Nickel (the 555th Combat Aviation coordinated our air transportation requirements) and get a bird in here for transportation back to Bear Cat. At least with prisoners we have a transportation priority, so we won't be stuck here long.

I thought Captain Sullivan would be really pissed, but the only thing he said was. "Sometimes you just got to do what you got to do." If there was any flak handed down for shipping the three VC soldiers back to Saigon, the Captain must have taken it, because he never said anything to me again about the incident.

The next two trips out to the bush went without any hang-ups and we managed to bring back a NVA officer, on the last trip. The Pros in Saigon were real happy about that one, and the unit that actually captured him got a unit citation out of the deal.

I had been back in Bear Cat for a day and a half and was spending my day off at the swimming pool just relaxing for a change. The next thing I see is Caffey, in uniform, walking in my direction. It's obvious he's not coming for a swim, and I new immediately, this wasn't going to be good.

"Better get dressed, *El Capitan* wants to see you, *deedee.*"

"Do you know what it's about?" I asked, knowing he wouldn't tell me, even if he knew. I know Caffey doesn't have much of a poker face, so I thought, I might at least get a hint of what the Captain wanted.

"I figured you'd know, they treat me like a mushroom around here, you know, they keep me in the dark and feed me shit."

"Not a clue." I said, unable to gain any useful information from observing Caffey's expression. Either he doesn't know what the Captain wants, or he is getting better at poker.

The ride back to the office didn't take long and my mind was occupied with trying to figure out if I had done something wrong. When we arrived I knocked on the Captain's door and it was opened by Big M.

"Have a seat Whitley." Captain Sullivan said and Morgan closed the door and stood against the wall.

"Did I do something wrong?"

"This is classified to the max, so listen up." The Captain said then Morgan took over.

"You are going after a special prisoner. A very special prisoner. A Chinese pilot, bailed out and was captured by a group of Cambodians. The local War Lord wants to sell him. That's all the information we have."

"Report to VE-AD. Colonel Augden's staff will brief you on details." The Captain said, then continued. "Tran is not going with you on this one. The powers that be want to keep this one as close to the vest as possible. Understand?"

"Yes Sir, I understand what you are telling me, but don't we have people that do this kind of stuff."

"What. You mean go after prisoners? Sure we do. You're it." The Captain said.

Well, that is not exactly what I meant, but I guess it was a stupid thing to ask. One of these days I'll learn to think before I ask dumb questions.

CHAPTER 3

Chesterfield Three Zero

Sergeant Williams dropped me off at the VE-AD compound. On the way to Saigon he asked me what was going on, and I told him that I really didn't know, and I was just following orders. SFC Williams had been around the detachment long enough to know not to pursue it, so he just dropped me off and went on his way to take care of some business in Saigon.

I made my way down the hall to Colonel Augden's office and knocked on the door. When I went in, my heart sank.

"Have a seat Sergeant Whitley. You know Jack Roark, don't you?"

"Yes Sir. I've had the pleasure."

"Well, Jack says you are the man for this job, so I'll let him explain it."

"Have a seat Whitley, this is going to take some time.

I sat down and knew this was not going to be good. I just knew it in my heart and wish I had never met this man, and in an instant visualized in my mind everything that has gone wrong since I first laid eyes on Jack Roark at the American Embassy in Germany.

Roark went to the map on the wall and started talking while pointing at the map. "You'll join a MACV-SOG Hatchet Force here at Dak To and proceed to Kong My in Laos to meet up with General Vang Pao and his Meo tribesmen. The reason we are using General Vang is because he has contacts with the Cambodian War Lord, Cam Ti. The word that filtered back to Kontum, is that Cam Ti's men captured a Chinese MIG 17 pilot that bailed out after a pair of F4 Phantoms went after two MIG 17s as targets of opportunity. They shot down one MIG 17 and damaged the other with Sidewinder missiles. The Phantoms were then jumped by two MIG 21s and bugged out, but not before losing one of the Phantoms. This has all been confirmed by Air Operations out of Thailand and the surviving F4 crew that was debriefed in Da Nang, so confidence is high that Cam Ti does have the pilot form the second MIG 17."

"You said, this Cam Ti wants to sell the pilot. Why wouldn't he just turn him over to the North Vietnamese?" I asked with some hesitancy

"Cam Ti is a drug War Lord. His motivation is money and knows he can't get shit out of the North Vietnamese. The only reason to even keep the pilot alive is to sell him to us. Believe me, we want him. This is proof that China is supplying MIG pilots to the North Vietnamese." Colonel Augden said, then continued. "Somebody give me a cigarette."

I took out a pack of Pall Malls and offered one to the Colonel, but he passed mine and took one of Roark's Salem's. "So I buy him, and then what? I mean how do I get him out of Cambodia?"

"You let CCC (SOG Command and Control Central) at Kontum work that out. Whitley, I want you to understand, that when you get this guy, he goes to Kontum, not back to the 525th Intelligence Group in Saigon. Understand?" Roark emphasized that point.

"No problem here on where he goes. Kontum just means I get rid of him sooner. I do have a question though. What do I buy this guy with?"

"Gold." Colonel Augden said.

"Gold?" I looked at Augden for clarification.

"Yes Gold." Augden said again as he placed two belts on the table. Then continued. "Each belt contains thirty South African one ounce gold pieces. General Vang will expect twenty of them, that's his usually fee. In any case do what ever it takes to get the job done."

Colonel Augden continued. "These are sealed classified orders to the Commander at CCC, they cover what I've just told you, so you shouldn't have any problems, and these are your travel orders to Kontum. Questions?"

"Just about the nuts and bolts." I said knowing I had a million questions that I haven't even thought about, but the main question being, *why me.* At least I knew the answer to that one had to be Jack Roark.

"Well, you let CCC work out the operation plan, they're the experts at this kind of stuff. If that's it, you better get started, my driver will take you to Tan Son Nhut."

With that, I picked up the sealed envelope and my travel orders and started out the door.

"Sergeant Whitley, aren't you forgetting something?" Augden asked.

"Sir?" I said as I turned around and looked at him.

"The gold, Sergeant, the gold."

"Oh, yes sir, the gold." I said and pick up the belts one at a time and put them around my waist under my jungle fatigues, then started to leave again.

"Sergeant, aren't you forgetting something else?"

"Yes sir, I'm sorry." I said then stood at attention and saluted, even though Colonel Augden was wearing civilian clothes.

"Not that Sergeant Whitley. You have to sign for that gold."

"Right. Of course, sign for the gold." I said and signed the receipt that Augden pushed across the desk, then left the office.

"Are you sure this is the right man for the job? He seems a little squirrelly to me." Augden questioned Roark.

"Yeah, I know. We could have just sent the Hatchet force in, but he's a good kid and he needs the experience. Besides, we need our man in there, who'll do what we tell him and keep his mouth shut. Who knows what might come up in the future." Roark replied.

Well I arrived at Tan San Nhut and had to hang out for about three hours before I caught a C47 going to Da Nang then on to the Special Forces camp at Kontum by helicopter. I knew the crew chief, Murphy, or at least had flown with him before. It was getting late when I reported in to the CCC, Command and Control Central, headquarters. I told the Spec Five at the desk in the office that I had sealed orders for the Commander.

The SP5 got up from his desk and went to the Commander's door, knocked, then poked his head in and said. "Sir, there's a spook out here that says he has sealed orders for you. Looks like trouble to me, sir."

"Well, send him in." Came the voice from the office.

The sign on the door read Lt. Col. Sellers, SOG CCC, Commanding Officer. The SP5 pushed the door open then stepped back. I walked passed him and reported to Colonel Sellers and handed him the envelope.

Sellers opened the envelope and began to read the orders then said. "Jake, go find the Sergeant Major, and shut the door on the way out." He continued reading and finally said. "Go ahead and have a seat Whitley. This is going to take a day or so to put together. I never thought when I passed this rumor on in my intel report that they would take it serious. At least now I know someone reads those things." "Do you really think this Chinese pilot exist?"

"Sir, I was told that the information was corroborated by Air Ops in Thailand and the surviving Phantom crew in Da Nang."

"That's not what I asked. Do you think he exist?"

"Sir, I just do what I'm told." I said just as the door was knocked on and opened.

"Sergeant Major, good, come on in." Sellers said then addressed the SP5. "Jake take Whitley over to the headquarters team hooch and find him a bunk."

I got up to follow Jake out of the office when the Colonel said. "If you want to leave the gold, I'll put in my safe."

"Yes sir, thank you." I said and was glad to get the extra weight off my hips.

On the way out the door the Sergeant Major said. "You can loose those collar pins, the men around here don't wear rank."

"Yes Sergeant Major." I said and continued to follow Jake.

The team hooch was just like the building I lived in, with sandbags halfway up the outside walls. The inside was open, not roomed off except for the two rooms at the end of the building. There was about twenty bunks in the squad bay all with the mosquito nets hanging from the rafters and a row of ceiling fans going down the center. A lot of mementos and souvenirs hung on the walls including a few Playboy magazine centerfolds and an Ann Margret poster. Some of the wall lockers had personal photos on them, and others just a piece of masking tape with names written on them. Jake pointed to one of the bunks and said take that one, he's not going to need it any more then walked over and pulled the name tape off the wall locker. "You might as well get a nap, chow is not for another hour." With that, Jake left the building. There wasn't anyone else in the hooch so I took my shirt off and laid down to catch a quick nap.

I dozed off for about twenty minutes or so, and when I woke up there was four guys in the hooch and they were stripping off field gear and soon headed out to the shower with towels wrapped around their necks. One of the guys spoke to me, more or less just to acknowledge my presents. At chow no one spoke to me except Jake. I don't think it was meant to be rude to me, and I could tell right away that these guys are real cliquish and not looking for any new friends. The Sergeant Major was right, no one was wearing any rank and most didn't even have name tags or US Army on there uniforms, if you could call them uniforms, they all looked a little ratty to me. I assumed they were Special Forces because of the painted wooden green beret on the building outside the mess hall, and the green beret I had seen in the hooch with a 5th Special Forces Group flash on it.

The Sergeant Major came by the table while I was eating and told me to be in the Old Man's office at 1000 hours tomorrow. He didn't join me, he just kept walking and sat down at another table with some of the other guys.

That night the guys put a couple of field tables together, threw a poncho liner over them and started playing poker. I wasn't invited to play, so I just hit the shower then went to sleep. About 0200 hours I was awakened by some booming off in the distance. At first I thought it was thunder, but then some more and the hooch was vibrating.

One of the guys rolled over in his bunk and saw me bolt up-right in mine, and said. "Ark Light."

"What's that, Ark Light, I mean?"

"B52s, that's all, nothing to worry about." He said then rolled back over.

I finally went back to sleep then l was awakened again. This time with louder booms, much closer, but I knew what they were. Out going artillery, probably 105mm howitzers. In between the cannon fire I heard something else, a different kind of booms, mortars. I wasn't the only one in the hooch that heard them. Every one jumped up grabbed their gear and started heading to the back door of the hooch, between the two rooms. As I got almost to the back door, the door of one of the rooms opened and the Sergeant Major grabbed me and said.

"Slow down there son, you'll hurt your self running in the dark, especially since you don't know where you're going." About that time the generators went out and so did the lights. I followed the Sergeant Major to the bunker.

A couple of minutes after we got there mortars were still coming-in and our artillery was still pounding away. Some one came to the entrance of the bunker and said the reaction force was ready and I heard the Sergeant Major say. "Well get after them." The mortars finally stopped after a few minutes, our artillery went silent a few minutes later. Another ten minutes went by then I heard someone blowing a whistle and the guys in the bunker started getting up and moving out, about that time I heard the generators start back up. On the way back to the hooch I asked one of the guys if this stuff happened every night. The response I got was, "Not every night, I remember one night last month, it was pretty quiet." I think he was joking, but I wasn't sure.

The next morning at chow, Jake came over and sat down at the table with me. "When you get done eating, I'll take you over to the supply room to get you geared up. Then the Colonel wants to see you."

At the supply room, I turned-in the gear I brought with me, including my steel pot, flak jacket and 45 cal. pistol. The Supply Sergeant said the 45 would never hold up, where I was going, and said he would return my gear if I made it back, and I don't think he was kidding. I drew a back pack and harness, four extra pairs of socks, an extra pair of jungle boots, a boonie hat, a set of camo fatigues with no patches what-so-ever on them, not even the US Army tape, a poncho and a camo poncho liner, a mosquito net (smaller than the ones we used to cover the bunks, but made out of the same material) a first aid kit, two olive drab towels, and a assortment of insect repellent, camo paint, and talcum powder.

I thought I was done, so I started filling the back pack, but I was wrong. The Sergeant then put on the counter three plastic bottles of pills. He picked one up, shook it and said.

"Salt tablets." Then picked another one up and said. "Uppers, be careful with these, they'll give you energy and keep you awake, but too many of them and you will crash, and this one is water purification pills. If you don't know how they work, it's one pill per full canteen, shake and wait at least two minutes before drinking. Taste like shit, but they'll keep you from catching the *Saigon two step*."

Not finished yet, the Sergeant kept piling stuff on the counter. Two more loaded M16 magazines to go with the three I already had and an extra ammo pouch for my pistol belt. He then put down a belt of 7.62mm ammo for a M60 machine gun, and thank heaven he didn't give me the machine gun to go with it. Jake clipped the ends of the M60 belt together so it could it could be worn over the shoulder like a Mexican bandito. The next item was the ugliest revolver I have ever seen. It was a 38 special with the bluing long gone, it was kind of a rusty brown color except for the barrel and cylinder which were stainless steel. Twenty five rounds of ammo for the pistol and a box of twelve energy food bars, and a machete in a scabbard. Finally he stopped, and Jake organized the pack for me and hooked it to the harness along with my pistol belt.

It was time to see Colonel Sellers. I left my gear with Jake and knocked on the commander's door. It was opened by the Sergeant Major.

"Come on in here Whitley and have a seat." Sellers said then the Sergeant Major chimed in.

"Have you ever been in the bush before?"

"No Sir, not really. Just to fly in and pick up prisoners."

"Oh, that's fuckin' great!" Said one of the other two soldiers in the room.

"Whitley this is Mike Brown and Jeff Junkins two of the guys that are going to take you in." Sellers said and I nodded in their direction.

The other man, Junkins, spoke up. "Are you sure you're up to this? I mean, we have a four or five day hump to get where we're going. This ain't going to be no fuckin' picnic."

"Oh he'll make it. Won't you son?" The Sergeant Major said more than asked, but I answered him anyway.

"Yes Sir, I'll make it." I said trying to convince myself as much as them.

"OK. Let's get to it." Sellers said then continued. "First of all, there is no way I'm sending in a Hatchet force. Just too many men, so you will go in with a modified Spike team, that would be best for this mission. You'll fly to Dak To on the border and pick up the rest of the team. Then you'll fly on to Kong Mi in Laos to hook up with General Vang Pao. His little army consist of mainly Meo tribesmen, but he also has a Company of mercenaries made up of Cambodian, Laotian, and Vietnamese deserters and ex-soldiers. Get the General paid off. Try to get four or five of his Meo tribesmen then send the like number of your Nung back to Dak To. OK so far?"

Brown spoke up. "You said a modified Spike team. How modified?"

"Modified only in that some of your Nungs will be replaced by Vang's men. Anything else?" No reply came so Sellers continued. "From Kong Mi, you'll have to hump it. Arrange for Vang's men to guide you across the border into Cambodia, but stay well clear of the Ho Chi Minh trail, I don't want you caught up in an Arc Light strike. Once you are in Cam Ti's territory, hold up and send two of Vang's men in to make contact. If everything is OK, then you make your deal with Cam Ti, after you verify that this guy is alive. We're not paying for a dead Chinaman. Questions so far?"

"OK. If a miracle happens and every thing goes the way it's suppose to. How do we get out? It will be too dangerous trying to go out the way we went in." Brown asked.

"That's right Mike. SOP (Standard Operating Procedure) says that you never go back the way you went in, because someone may have spotted you or your trail and given that information to the North Vietnamese and nobody, including Mrs. Brown, wants her baby boy to walk into an ambush. Now, can we let the Colonel continue." The Sergeant Major said in a manner bordering on sarcasm. Then Sellers continued.

"You'll be out of range of normal radio communication but you should be in range of the ASA radio listing post in the triangle, call sign Pluto. They won't talk back to you but they'll relay any message you have back here. Your call sign is Chesterfield Three Zero, the freq is 5555. If we need to get a message to you, we'll have to use aircraft on the rescue channel. Now to answer Mike's question. Whether you have the pilot or not, you have four exit plans. Alpha, make your way to the Mekong here." The Colonel pointed to a point on the map and continued. "It will take you a day and a half hump and a PBR (Patrol Boat, River.) will pick you up. Bravo, due east two days, but you'll have to be damn careful, you will cross the Ho Chi Minh trail in several places. Wouldn't be my first pick. Anyway you should cross the border between these two ridges." Again the Colonel pointed to a position on the map. While Junkins marked the points on his map.

"Charlie, is an air extraction, very dangerous, we have lost a lot of aircraft in that area and officially we are not even in Cambodia. Also dangerous because they will have to carry extra fuel with them, that means an extended period on the ground while they refuel. Send a message when you reach Cam Ti's area, again when the deal goes down, green for go and red for no deal, and identify your exit, Alpha, Bravo or Charlie. After that a status report every 12 hours. Just another walk in the park. Any questions?"

I know, don't ask any dumb questions, but I just can't help myself. "Yes Sir, you said there were four exit plans?"

Mike Brown spoke up and said. "Plan Delta, we get out any fuckin' way we can. Right Sergeant Major?"

"That's right Mike, any way you can. OK gear up, your bird to Dak To leaves at 1300 hours. Pick up the rest of the team and you should be in General Vang's camp in Kong Mi by 1600 hours."

Was I scared? Well if I wasn't, I was doing a pretty good impression of it and had no doubt that I would know for sure before this trip was over.

CHAPTER 4

The Hump

We picked up the fourth American on the team at Dak To, a Special Forces linguist and medic named Carl Muchinhaus, Muchie for short. We also picked up 8 CIA trained Nung tribesmen armed with a M60 machine gun, two M79 grenade launchers and shotguns, all had machetes and belts of ammo crisscrossed over their shoulders. Sergeant Hoc, the leader of the Nungs came up to me and pointed to the ammo belt I was carrying and Muchie said.

"Give it to him, they love that M60, it's like a status symbol to them."

Well I certainly had no problems with that, I have never carried so much stuff in my life, although it seemed like everyone else was carrying more than me. Mike Jones was our communications guy, so besides his gear he was also backpacking a radio, and Muchie also had his medical kit. Jeff Junkins the leader of our expedition was carrying a different kind of radio, a small crystal controlled short wave, that we would send messages to Pluto with. I say Jeff was the leader, it was my mission, but there was no question that Jeff was in charge. Me, well, the only reason I can figure out, that I am going is to protect the interest of Jack Roark and Colonel Augden, who want to make sure they get credit for capturing this Chinese pilot, if he even exist. Colonel Sellers made it perfectly clear that he thought this whole thing was a snipe hunt, but like the rest of us, he follows his orders to the best of his ability.

With the M60 ammo I was carrying, handed over to Sergeant Hoc, the only thing extra I was carrying was 60 ounces of gold around my waist. Fortunately, I was about to get rid of a bunch of it.

We left Dak To on schedule, in three Hueys courtesy of the Jokers, 48th AHC, a slick with the Nungs and Muchie on board. Brown, Junkins and I rode on one of the two gun ships. Shortly after crossing the border into Laos we started taking some machine gun and other small arms fire. The bird we were on and the slick with the Nungs immediately did a u-turn, while the second gun ship dealt with the problem. Soon we were back on course and on our way to Kong Mi.

We received no further fire from the ground and landed safely in Laos. The Meo tribesmen were suitably impressed with our Nung warriors, the General on the other hand was going to play hard to get. We had to wait while a meal of monkey meat, fruit, and rice with that ever present Nuoc mam (fish sauce) was prepared, which is the custom, and we were not allowed to talk with the General until the meal was over.

The meal wasn't as bad as it sounds, except for the duck eggs with dead embryos in them and thankfully the Laotian style of Nuoc mam isn't as offensive to the nose as the Vietnamese style. After the meal, negotiations with General Vang Pao started with Jeff and me on one side, Muchie doing the translating, and the General and three of his officers on the other. The twenty gold coins was not the problem, 20 ounces of gold is his going rate as an ally of ours. The problem is that he only wants to provide one of his men to guide us and not the five that we wanted. He also wants to be paid two more gold coins for the man, one for the General and one for the man's family.

After about 15 minutes of belches from the dinner and three or four cups of rice wine we concluded the negotiations and agreed on two of his Meo tribesmen to guide us, for which the General is to be paid 5 gold coins, twenty five in all. I excused myself by telling the General I had to return to one of the helicopters to get his gold. Inside the Huey I removed five coins from one of the belts, placed them in the other and returned that belt to my waist under my fatigue shirt. The pilot of one of the birds wanted to know how much longer they had to stay, he said they had to be back before dark. I told him we were almost done.

The General was happy with his gold, and I was happy to be rid of almost half of what I was carrying. Jeff decided not to send any of the Nung back to Dak To, and released the helicopters. We spent the night in two groups sleeping on raised platforms that had thatch type roofs covering them while the Nung took turns standing guard. Little did I know then that this would be the best nights sleep and the best meal I would have in the foreseeable future.

With daylight, we set off on our expedition, being led by two Meo dressed in their traditional garb and armed with hand made crossbows, blowguns stuck in their belts, and large flat knives that came to a squared off end with a hook on one side, that they used like machetes and slashed through the ever encumbering brush. It is pointless to tell you that I was exhausted, I was in sheer misery after the first ten minutes, but there was no option other than to keep up and keep putting one boot in front of the other.

After the first hour, my body started going numb from this slow uphill slug through the brush. It was actually a relief, as I couldn't feel the pain of my pack and harness cutting through my shoulders anymore. We stopped frequently to drink water while one of the guides scouted forward. The second time we stopped, Muchie came over and pushed my pack up and adjusted my harness for me. He also gave me a salt tablet and an upper to take. No one spoke while we were traveling, only the occasional whispers between Jeff, Muchie and the guides.

After about four hours the brush thinned a little and the trees started getting taller as we approached the top of the hill we have been climbing. Just over the ridgeline we moved down to the last stand of forest cover. Below us was a valley covered with rice paddies and a small stream running through the middle of the valley with what looked like a small village just to the west.

Jeff huddled us all together and said that we were going to stop for a while, then explained what was going on.

"There is enough moon tonight, so we'll move down and cross the stream and rice paddies at 2400 hours. After we cross the stream we'll be in Cambodia and will follow it down stream until it joins the river about three clicks away." Jeff pointed to our position on the map then continued. "We'll stay on the west side of the river and head south until daylight, then we'll have to hold up for a while."

At last a break. We stayed just inside the wood line on the side of the hill and I survived the first day, at least I thought I had. Once I sat down and dropped my pack, I realized I must actually be dead because I couldn't move. I was out for about an hour when Muchie woke me and told me to eat something and change my socks. We didn't start a fire because it could have been seen from across the valley. The Nungs and Meo were eating cold rice and dried fish they had brought with them. I got a couple of the energy bars out of my pack and started to eat one when Sergeant Hoc came over to me with a leaf containing some rice and fish. After he pointed a

Ronald E. Whitley

couple of times I realized he wanted to trade for one of my bars.

After we ate, Hoc sent three of his men out to replace the look-outs he had posted. Mike Brown came over and sat down beside me and said. "We've got about four hours, better get some sleep."

Mike took the net material out of his pack, pulled over his jungle hat and covered his face and neck, then tucked it into his fatigues. So with his M16 between his legs he leaned back on his pack and went to sleep. I did the same.

I don't know how long it was, but it wasn't long enough, when Jeff came by and told us to grease up and get ready to move out in 10 minutes. Mike was putting camo paint on his face, so I followed his lead. Muchie came by and reminded us to take salt tablets and offered me a couple of aspirin. We were just getting ready to head down into the valley when we could see, hear and feel multiple explosions coming from down stream toward the river. It was a B52 strike on Uncle Ho's trail. It was so terrifying that I found myself holding on to the ground to keep from bouncing down the hillside. We were over three miles away and I can't even imagine what it must be like to be under that kind of devastation. It felt like an earthquake and seemed to go on for several minutes.

We waited about twenty minutes to make sure the bombing was over then headed down the hill and out across the rice paddies. When we crossed the stream, we took the opportunity to fill our canteens, then crossed more paddies to the edge of a wood line and turned to follow the stream to the river. When we got to the river we headed east to follow the flow of the water. Where the stream entered the river there was a small hamlet that we had to ease our way around. Once around and clear of the hamlet we could see fires still burning on the other side of the river and even hear the occasional scream.

We continued on until daylight then stopped and waited for the guides to scout ahead. We changed socks and boots and when they returned we continued on for about another mile then stopped in what look like an abandon village that had been mostly burned out some time ago. Not far from the village was an old stone shrine with faces, heads, dragons and snakes carved into the stone blocks. It didn't look that big at first, until you realized that most it was covered by jungle. We hadn't seen any signs of local life for over two hours so we stopped to take a long break. Jeff said it was safe enough to build a cooking fire. The Nungs cooked their rice and Mike made some coffee and one of the guides gathered some fruit from the jungle. After we ate and rested for a couple of hours we headed out again. That evening the moon was covered by clouds most of the time so we stopped for the night in the jungle line just back from the river shore.

The next morning we got ready to make the push that would take us into Cam Ti's area. My body was racked with pain and I could barely move, but I knew my muscles would loosen up once we got started. I took a salt tablet, an upper, and a couple of aspirin, washed it down with the last of my water. Mike and three of the

Nung gathered our canteens and went to the river while Jeff sent the two guides ahead.

A minute or two went by then there was a lot of yelling followed by some gunfire. First it was AK47 fire in multiple short burst then M16 fire and more yelling. I could hear Mike screaming something, but I couldn't make it out. I headed in the direction of the river and was passed by three of the Nung soldiers. There was more AK47 fire, but the M16 fire had stopped. Then I heard two thuds from the M79s being fired, a second or two later the two explosions, then nothing. By the time I got to the river bank, Mike and one of the Nung were being dragged by Muchie and Sergeant Hoc in my direction. Muchie looked briefly at Mike then went to where Sergeant Hoc was working frantically on the wounded Nung. Muchie put his hand on Hoc's back and said.

"He's gone, Hoc, he's gone." Then returned to Mike Brown. Mike was in pain and mumbling incoherently. "Easy Mike, you're OK, you're going to be fine, it's just your hand, you're going to be OK."

"What the hell happened?" Jeff asked Muchie as he bent down to check on Mike.

"They went to get water and the man that was supposed to be the lookout wasn't paying attention, and a sampan slipped up on them. Probably thought they were fishermen until they spotted Mike and the weapons. Then all hell broke loose. Mike's M16 was shot out of his hand, the round hit the gun, but a fragment went through his hand."

"How's the other man." Jeff asked.

"He's gone." Was all Muchie said.

Jeff went down to the river, and not seeing or hearing any commotion on the other side, picked up what was left of Mike's M16 and threw it in the river and picked up the filled canteens. By this time there was nothing left of the sampan, just a couple of bodies floating down river. When he returned he said.

"Damn it to hell, if we don't stay awake and keep sharp we're all going to get zapped." Then walked over to where Hoc was crying over the dead man.

"He was my younger brother." Hoc said still sobbing.

"I know Hoc, and I'm sorry, but we have to burry him and get out of here."

"I know, I know, but he was my brother." Hoc said as he started taking the man's gear off.

After the dead man was buried in the jungle to keep the grave from being found, and Mike's hand was bandaged and on his feet, we got ready and headed out. Following the guide that had returned to get us.

We followed the river for about another mile then headed into a thickly forested area. Two hours later as the forest thinned we came in sight of a small hamlet and a Buddhist temple that we had to skirt our way around. We were entering Cam Ti's area and only a mile or two from where we would wait for the Meo tribesmen to make contact.

CHAPTER 5

The Chinese Pilot

After we stopped for the wait, we tried to make contact on Mike's radio with no luck, so we unpacked the short wave that Jeff had carried. After the antenna wires were strung up in a couple of trees and one of the Nung cranking the handle on the little generator. Jeff tapped out in slow deliberate Morse code the following message.

"Pluto this is Chesterfield three zero, message for Tiger Charlie six, reached papa one, one kilo and one whisky, will continue." Then repeated the message two more times. We took the opportunity to rest while Jeff sent the two Meo to make contact with Cam Ti. While I was changing my socks, Muchie came by and lanced the blisters on my feet and sprinkled them with antiseptic powder.

"Now you know where the term tenderfoot comes from. You should have told me about the blisters sooner." Muchie said.

"I didn't want to bother you with so much going on, Mike and all. How's he doing?"

"As you can see, he's holding his own. I couldn't slow him down even if I wanted to. He wouldn't even let one of the Nung pack his radio. If I can keep that hand from getting infected, he'll be OK."

"How long does Jeff say we'll be here?"

"He doesn't know, we just have to wait for the Meo to make contact and lead us in. Get something to eat and get some rest."

"Thanks Muchie." I said, put my boots back on, lit a cigarette and leaned back. Soon I was asleep.

I don't know how long it was, but the next thing I remember was Sergeant Hoc shaking me and saying. "They back, they back."

The Meo had brought back one of Cam Ti's soldiers with them, and we were soon on our way. About twenty minutes in to the hump there was some commotion behind me, and we all stopped. One of the Nung had been bit by a snake. Muchie worked on him and gave him a shot of anti venom while a litter was being made out of two sapling trees and a couple of ponchos. Muchie said it was bad, but he had a chance, so he was loaded on the litter and we continued. An hour and forty minutes or so later we arrived at Cam Ti's base camp.

If Cam Ti was a Cambodian there must be something else in the mix, because he was a big, imposing man with a sparse scraggily beard, twice the size of the average Cambodian. The man that was snake bit was taken into one of the huts where some Cambodian women went to work on him. Muchie watched, I guess he figured they knew more about snakebites than he did. In the same hut was the Chinese pilot with two broken legs that had been set with bamboo splints.

"Americans, are you Americans? Oh my God am I glad to see you guys. I didn't think anyone was ever going to come for me."

Muchie and I just stood there dumbfounded for a moment as he kept asking question after question with tears running down his face.

Oh he was a Chinese pilot alright, his name was Tommy Chang, from Lancaster, California, USA. Captain Chang wasn't the Mig17 pilot as reported, in fact he had been the back seat in the F4 Phantom that had been shot down. Muchie took his medical bag and went to check him out. Actually he was in pretty good shape for someone that had been shot down, bailed out, broke both his legs during the ejection and landed in the jungle. I went to find Jeff and give him the news.

Jeff and I decided it was not important to try and explain to Cam Ti the difference in what he was holding. Just get on with the negotiations and get the hell out of here.

We had underestimated Cam Ti, he knew exactly what he had. He figured that if he had reported that he had an American pilot, we would have just came in force and taken him. I don't know if he was right or not, but I certainly understood his point of view. Also, he didn't want gold, he had a list of supplies he wanted, and he figured he could bargain with a small force sent in to get a Chinese pilot. Cam Ti didn't exactly lie in his report, he just shrewdly left out the fact that his Chinese pilot was an American.

The supplies he wanted was 200 pounds of rice, 100 cartons of Salem cigarettes, 2 cases of Jack Daniel's whisky, and 150 4.2 inch mortar rounds. He figured that is what an American pilot is worth and didn't want to haggle about it.

Jeff, Mike and I devised a message to send that would be understood without telling the whole world what was going on. This is what we came up with.

"Pluto this is Chesterfield three zero, relay to Tiger Charlie six, message follows, green light, package not as expected, package is Yankee Doolittle Dandy with broken wheels, urgent contact by aircraft for exchange requirements. Be advised Alpha and Bravo not an option, must be Charlie."

Jeff set up to send the message and he ask me if I thought they would understand the part about *Yankee Doolittle Dandy*. Someone would, I said then went back to tell Captain Chang that plans for his evac were under way and get some more information from him.

Tommy Chang said he had been the rear seat on the number four bird with Major Bledsoe, in a flight that had been on a SAM suppression mission and had taken a little flak, flyable but had slowed them down, the number three bird, Bleeder one three, stayed with them while one and two, out of missiles continued on to Da Nang. That's when they spotted the two Mig 17s, since they still had some missiles left they went after them. One three got the first Mig, then we nailed the other. That's when the Mig21s showed up. The Phantoms don't have guns and we were out of missiles, so we bugged out. One of the Migs got in a lucky burst from their guns that hit the right wing ripping a hole in it and tearing off the tip of the wing. Chang said they went out of control and Major Bledsoe yelled "Eject, eject, eject". Chang hit something on the way out loosing his survival kit and never did see Bledsoe's chute. The next thing he knew he thought he had been captured, but it turned out to be Cam Ti's men who brought him into camp set his legs, and have been taking care of him. He said that between the Chinese he learned from his grand parents and what little Vietnamese he knows he has been trying to communicate with them but hasn't had much luck.

"OK Captain, we're working on getting you out of here. Can you tell me your flight number and call sign."

"Yeah sure. We were Bleeder one four, and my call sign is Dragon." He managed a laugh and said. "I didn't pick it, that's what they gave me, at least it wasn't Eggroll or something stupid like that."

Muchie came in to check on the snakebite. The man was running a fever and was delirious. One of the woman had made some tea out of local herbs and was giving it to him a little at a time.

Mike came in to get his bandage changed and said. "What is that stuff they're giving him?"

"I don't know, but it can't hurt, there's nothing more I can do, except get him out of here to a hospital." Muchie said while unwrapping Mike's hand. "Christ, I was afraid of this, that shit is getting infected."

One of the older women came over and looked at Mike's hand and said something in Cambodian. "She says she has something for that hand." Muchie said.

The old woman went to her baskets and got two small leaves, a piece of bark a small root and with a small amount of water, started grinding the concoction up in to a paste. The old woman mumbled something and Muchie told Mike to open his hand.

"Are you sure she knows what she's doing?" Mike questioned.

"These people have been doing their own doctoring for hundreds of years, besides, I don't have anything left to give you."

The old woman got some of the paste and placed it into his palm and rolled his hand up into a fist. She then brought a jar over and pulled out a leach and applied it to the back of his hand, then repeated the procedure with a second and third leach. The Cambodian woman then gave the instruction to Muchie.

"She said to leave the leaches on till they fall off, they will suck the *Mukgok* through the wound."

"Muchie, I think you've gone native on us, that's the dumbest shit I've ever heard."

"Well, it may be, but I've got to try something to control the infection. I damn sure don't want to do my first field amputation. Cheer up Mike, I was just fuckin' with you. You'll probably be in a hospital before the day is over with."

Less than two hours had passed when we heard jets screaming over head and started doing a wide circle above us. Mike's radio finally cracked to life.

"Ground unit from Eagle Leader. Do you copy, over."

"Get that Mike said to me." As he held his hand up.

"I'll get Jeff." Muchie said on his way out the door.

I got the radio handset that was clipped to Mike's harness and answered the call. "Eagle Leader, this is ground unit, copy you loud and clear."

"OK ground, I've got you, can you identify yourself."

"Eagle Leader, this is Chesterfield three zero."

"If we understand your message correctly, you have a damaged package, can you identify?"

"Roger, Eagle Leader, I identify as Bleeder one four, call sign Dragon."

Muchie and Jeff had entered the hut and were listing.

"Understand Chesterfield, confirm you only have one package."

Jeff took over the radio and confirmed that we only had one package but we had three wounded total and ten others for extraction. Then went on to give the list of supplies that Cam Ti wanted for the exchange. Eagle Leader confirmed the information that Jeff had given him and said it would take some time and someone would be back in contact. Then the jets vanished.

Another four hours went by, then a single jet flew over head and made radio contact. The supply drop and extraction would not take place until daylight tomorrow. It would be a long night as Cam Ti's guest.

Later on that evening, the snakebite victim's fever was coming down, and his leg stopped swelling. Muchie said that if we can get him to a hospital tomorrow, he will probably be alright. Sergeant Hoc went to Jeff and told him that some of the Nung were getting nervous, they were afraid that if the drop didn't come off as scheduled, Cam Ti would have his men kill them. We were outnumbered about twenty-five to one, but so far Cam Ti seems to be confident that the Americans will deliver his mortar rounds and the other stuff he wanted. If not he would loose face among his men if he didn't do something. I didn't put much stock into it until I remembered the guy is just a drug king pin with a private army, and who knows what he would do if he thinks he's been double-crossed.

The long night was interrupted by gunfire in the jungle not far from the base camp. There was a lot of activity in camp with Cam Ti's men scurrying about. Finally a patrol left camp. We had no idea what was going on and the Nung were really on edge. An hour or so later there was more gunfire. It was a long night.

As daylight slowly started to break, every ear was tuned to the sky listing for aircraft, but the only thing that could be heard was more gunfire coming from the direction of the river. Finally I heard Jeff on the radio with someone, I couldn't make out what was being said, just then two A1 Skyraiders buzzed the camp and started circling. Jeff went out to the small clearing in the center of the camp and popped a red smoke grenade. Within two minutes we could hear the rumble of a HH3, Jolly Green Giant, with a pallet slung underneath coming in to view of the camp. The Jolly Green came to a hover then slowly descended until his pallet was on the ground. Once Jeff unhooked the supplies the helicopter moved forward and landed but kept his engine on. Muchie and I got the wounded ready to load, but our way was blocked by some of Cam Ti's men. Cam Ti finally signaled his men by waving a carton of Salem in one hand and a bottle of Jack Daniel's in the other. The Pararescueman and the Flight Engineer jumped out and helped us load Captain Chang and the snakebite victim. Then Mike with more leaches applied to his hand this morning still attached got aboard, followed by the rest of us.

More gunfire, closer now just on the edge of the camp. Cam Ti's men were firing into the jungle line and two other Skyraiders came into view and they were firing rockets and strafing what turned out to be a considerable size NVA force. As we became airborne, the two A1s that had been circling us, joined the fray firing rockets and guns. We headed north and gained altitude with one of the Skyraiders rejoining us. Finally Cam Ti's two mortars started firing. I guess he got his re-supply just in time. We took a few hits from small arms, but nothing serious. About two minutes into the flight we were joined by the other three Skyraiders, then turned to a north easterly heading.

I could see the river and some of the tributaries below us as we crossed them. It didn't take long and we were back over South Vietnam and our A1 Skyraider escort left us. The Flight Engineer got a couple of the Nung to start pumping the handles on two auxiliary fuel drums. I don't know if we are losing fuel or just starting to get low, but the Engineer didn't seem to be in a panic or anything, and I was just glad to be out of the jungle. Another forty minutes or so and we were landing at the Dak To airfield. Muchie and the wounded were put on a Dust-off Huey that was waiting and Jeff, Sergeant Hoc and I boarded another bird heading to Kontum.

After giving the Supply Sergeant all his dirty field gear back, I stripped down, slung the gold belt over my shoulder, grabbed a folding chair and walked naked to the shower room and just sat down under the water. I don't know how long I was there, maybe 20 minutes or so, finally the Sergeant Major came in carrying the gear

I had left with the Supply Sergeant when this little walk in the park started.

"Well son, you made it. I knew you had it in you. Ever think about joining the Special Forces?"

"Sergeant Major, no disrespect intended but if this is what you guys do for a living, well God bless you, but I think I'll pass."

"OK Whitley, shave and get dressed, the Colonel wants to debrief you before you leave."

I struggled getting dressed, every muscle in my body ached and I had lost about 10 pounds in five days. In Lt. Colonel Sellers' office, I told him my version of what happened on the mission and he reminded me that the mission was classified on a need to know basis. I was too tired and in too much pain to eat so I caught a C130 going to Tan Son Nhut. On the flight I thought about going to Bear Cat checking-in and getting about 24 hours sleep, then going to Saigon to see Colonel Augden. I knew I had to face Augden sooner or later so I decided to go to Saigon first, and get it over with. That way, at least I'll be able to get rid of the rest of this gold I have been packing around.

At the VE-AD compound I returned the remainder gold to Augden and told him the whole story. He seemed disappointed in the fact that it had not gone the way he wanted, and less interested in the fact that we actually rescued an Air Force pilot.

I got a ride to the APO, got something to eat while I waited, and rode back to Bear Cat in the afternoon mail truck. I figured I would get some sleep, then see the Captain tomorrow. I was wrong. I don't know how long I had been asleep, but it wasn't long enough, and I was awaken by Caffey banging on my door then letting himself in.

"Hey sleeping beauty, wake up, *El Capitan* wants to see you, *deedee*."

"Yeah, OK, I'll be there in a minute."

I got up and got dressed again, then went to the office.

"Set down Whitley before you fall down, I've got some bad news. Sergeant Franks and Mister Quan have been killed."

"Killed, what happened?"

"Helicopter crash, everyone on board was killed. So unless we get some more personnel, you will be spending a lot more time in the Delta. You'll have most of the area you have now in II Corps plus III Corps. You look like shit and I wish I could give you some time off, but I just don't see how that's possible right now."

"I understand Sir. Is that all?"

"In a minute. How did the mission go, did you get the Chinese pilot?"

"Yes Sir, I mean no Sir, will kind of." I said then gave Captain Sullivan the details on the mission. He remarked that he bet Colonel Augden wasn't too pleased and I confirmed his conjecture.

CHAPTER 6

The Mekong Delta

Well, I'm an old veteran now, been over two months since I arrived in-country and can't imagine doing nine more months of this crap, so I just don't think about it much. Tran and I along with our MP, Spec 4 David Feldman, the *Philly Flash,* were out on the tarmac at the airfield at Bear Cat early one morning waiting on a replacement Huey. The helicopter we were suppose to go out on had some kind of electrical problem, according to Murphy the Crew Chief. So while Murphy and our pilot went to sign out another bird. We were stuck listening to more of Feldman's wild stories and tall tales. He couldn't possibly have done ten percent of the things he claims, if he was fifty years old, but he wasn't fifty he is only eighteen and looks like he is about fifteen. Being with this kid makes me feel like an old man at the age of twenty one.

Finally I see Murphy waiving at us, so we head to the Huey he's standing next to. We load up while the pilot runs back to the airfield shack for something. When he gets back he does one last walk around then climes in. It is cold this morning, the sun is just starting to make it's appearance as I hear the click, click, click of the igniter box, then the slow whine of the turbine starting to gain momentum, and of course the familiar wop, wop, wop of the rotor blade, slowly at first then gradually increasing in speed until we are ready for takeoff.

It didn't take long for the sun to take control of the day and by the time we landed in Tan An, I was completely soaked. We made our way to the CP (Command Post), and were told our prisoners were actually at a temporary fire support position near Tan Tru. Tran tried to catch our bird, but they had already taken off to assist in the extraction of a LRRP unit (Long Range Recon Patrol) in the Plain of Reeds, so we were in for a very uncomfortable twenty minute truck ride to the prisoners.

Twenty minutes is what we were told, of course they didn't tell us that we would be stopped in the middle to let the engineers clear the road of mines. I was really uncomfortable looking out across the rice paddies, just sitting there in my own sweat, playing sniper target.

Our twenty minute ride took us about an hour and a half, which seemed like an eternity being stuck there with the Philly Flash, but we made it unscathed. The prisoners turned out to be a Viet Cong officer, or at least he claimed to be when Tran questioned him, and his radio man. Our helicopter was still tied up and we were told to make our way back to Tan An by vehicle and we would be met there.

About a mile out of Tan Tru, the M113 armored personnel carrier, the only track vehicle in our three vehicle convoy, was hit by an RPG. While the grunts were coming out of the back hatch it was hit again, then seconds later our truck was hit in the engine compartment making the ¾ ton truck's front end jump and slide nose first into the rice paddy. The machine gun mounted in the jeep behind us opened up, blasting across the paddy to the earthen walkway that separates the rice fields. He must have picked the right spot, because we started taking small arms fire from the same location. I had jumped out of the truck and was firing my M16 in the same direction and was soon joined by the four infantrymen that had managed to get out of the M113.

I stopped for a second to yell at Feldman who I noticed was still in the bed of the truck and not firing his weapon. I don't remember exactly what I yelled, but it was something about getting the prisoners out of the truck. The jeep that was behind us then took a hit from a RPG that was fired from the other side of the road. With the loss of the machine gun that was on the jeep, we were in deep shit and being fired upon from both sides of the road. Feldman finally dragged one of the prisoners off the back of the truck and took cover. I looked around for Tran but didn't see him, just then the machine gun mounted on top of the M113 came to life, and all I could think was thank God. With the machine gun keeping Charlie's head down on one side, we were able to concentrate our M16 fire on the other. I could hear a 50 cal. machine gun start firing but I couldn't tell where it was coming from. I did see mud and water flying up in the direction we were firing. I was completely out of M16 ammo when I heard helicopters over head.

The battle was soon over and we counted our dead and wounded. Eight dead, three from the M113, two from the jeep and three from our truck, the driver and the Staff Sergeant that was beside him, and one of our prisoners. Wounded we had five, including the Philly Flash that took a ricochet in the thigh and Tran who was badly burned. Tran was the one who made it inside the M113 and was firing the machine gun. The 50 cal. was fired from another M113 coming from Tan Tru, that should have been part of our convoy, but got held up. (Lucky them.) It seemed that the ambush and firefight lasted forever, but in fact the whole thing was over in just under ten minutes.

The infantry squad exited the second M113 and loaded up our wounded to return to Tan Tru and I sent the prisoner back with them. Eight of the infantrymen stayed with us to wait for the engineers coming from Tan An to clear the road. The Sergeant, who had been with the second M113, took four of his men and crossed the paddy to make a body count of the Viet Cong. When they reached the other side of the paddy, I heard three single shots from a M16 then I could see them starting back. They dropped off two AK47, three ChiCom rifles and a RPG, then went to do the same thing on the other side of the road.

I saw a Huey coming low across the rice paddies and landed on the road between us and Tan An. Murphy jumped out and came over to me and asked.

"You call for a taxi? What the hell happened here anyway?"

"We drove smack into an ambush. That's what. Charlie had us from both sides of the fuckin' road."

"Where's Tran and the other guy?"

"Both wounded, taken back to Tan Tru with the prisoner."

Then coming from the loud speaker on the Huey. "Murf, come on, we have a hot one."

"Come on, let's go, we need a gunner anyway." Murphy said and I followed him, running, both of us jumped on the bird.

Murphy plugged his head phones in and talked to the pilot while we were taking off, then took the gunners' helmet of the hook, plugged it in and handed it to me.

"Can you hear me OK?"

"OK." I said and gave him a thumbs-up as I fastened the chin strap.

"There's a unit about 30 clicks up in the Plain of Reeds that's calling for help. They have wounded and there's not a dust-off that's anywhere close. So we're it. Can you handle the M60?"

"Yeah, no problem." I said as I slid down in behind the door gun and checked the ammo can which was full.

"Hey be careful, we don't want to loose you." Murphy said as he bent down and strapped the tether harness on me. "An ARVN soldier slid out on one trip and they threatened to court marshal me. No telling what they do if I lost you." Murphy laughed, slapped me on the back then climbed unto the co-pilot seat.

Sometimes we had two pilots, but often as not there was only one. This trip there is only one. So with only three of us on board the bird we headed southwest. All I could think of was how beautiful everything is from the air. If I had my choice about things, this is what I'd do. I love flying. Too soon for me, the pilot was talking to the ground unit on the radio. Then on the intercom the said.

"Get that M60 ready, we are going to be going in hot."

The next thing I knew, we went in to a steep dive then into a wide sweeping turn to the right. I started hearing a plinking noise and it took me about a second to realize that we were being shot at. "Oh crap!" I heard the pilot say then he jerked the bird up sharply. Then an explosion just out side the helicopter and we went into a slow spin.

The next voice I heard on the intercom was Murphy. "Hang on, Bill has been hit and we lost the tail rotor." That was it, the next thing I knew I was out side the helicopter hanging on for dear life, screaming my ass off trying to pull myself back into the spinning bird with the tether harness. The ground was coming up fast as we were headed sideways into it. We hit hard and started flipping side over side. I hit hard back inside, hitting the deck then the top, then the deck again as we rolled over and over. Finally we stopped but I couldn't move. It took me a few seconds to realize that I was rapped up and tangled in the harness about a foot from the bottom which was actually the side of what was left of the bird. I then see Murphy crawling toward me with his knife out. Murphy starts cutting and I hit face first, then the rest of me crashes down.

"We've got to get the hell out of here." Murphy said, then he passed out. I shook him but he was out cold. Then I could see the gash in his flight suit covered with blood. All my arms and legs were working so I grabbed onto Murphy and started pulling him through the gapping hole in the bird. Just in time too, as soon as we cleared the wreck and got a little distance away, what was left of the wreck went up in flames. About thirty meters into the tall grass I stopped to look at Murphy's wound. It was a five inch gash in the upper thigh of his left leg. There were no arteries or anything cut, but it was still bleeding a lot. While I was tying a pressure bandage tightly around Murphy's leg is when I first noticed all the gun fire close to us and the occasional round come ripping through the grass. I thought about trying to go back and find my M16, but I remembered I didn't have any ammo for it. It didn't make any difference anyway, as just then the bird exploded.

I tried to revive Murphy, he was conscious but incoherent. The side of his helmet was cracked and there was several trickles of blood running down his neck. I was afraid if I took his helmet off to look, I would just make it worse. Murphy had just saved my life by cutting me loose, but I don't know for how long. I figured I was dead, I just haven't died yet, and now Murphy isn't going to make it, unless I can get my head out of my ass, find out what's going on and get him some help.

More rounds ripping through grass close to us drove me to make a move. I didn't think we were being shot at, but somebody is sure as hell shooting at somebody. I dragged Murphy closer to the firefight in hope that I could find the good guys. Almost too close now, I could hear voices and they weren't Americans. I left Murphy and crawled through the grass to see what I could figure out. Through the grass I could see seven or eight Viet Cong engaged in a firefight with three or four Americans from the sound of the M16 fire being returned. I crawled back to Murphy. He was more aware of what was going on, but still a little out of it. I told him that I was going to get help, but just incase, I got his pistol, checked it, and placed it in his hand.

I really didn't think I would be back, if Charlie didn't get me, I would probably be shot by the grunts shooting in their direction. I wouldn't be here if it wasn't for Murphy, and Murphy is the reason I have to try. Armed with only my 45 pistol, I crawled back through the grass to my previous location. This is the point that it becomes a little foggy to me. Later the Sergeant with the infantryman under fire told me he saw me stand up and start screaming like a banshee as I charged the Viet Cong killing several of them including the machine gunner, allowing them to advance and kill the remainder of the Cong.

"Hey! Hey! Are you OK?" The Sergeant said as he grabbed my right hand that was still trying to fire the 45 even though it was empty.

"Yeah, I'm OK. We've got to get to Murphy."

"Who's Murphy? Are you sure you're OK?"

"Yeah, I told you, I'm OK. Murphy is back there in the grass."

Two of the soldiers were carrying Murphy as the patrol headed back to the main unit, which itself was under heavy fire and almost surrounded. As we made our way back I noticed it cooled off a little and the sky was getting dark. That's when the sky opened up and it started to rain, and I mean rain hard. I could barely see a foot in front of myself as I heard the Sergeant yell out.

"It's Carvel, we're coming in."

One of the three medics with the unit went to work on Murphy and I was taken to Lieutenant Flores who was in charge, since the Captain was wounded and the XO, who was also the headquarters Platoon Leader, had been killed. Flores told me they were Bravo Company, 6th of the 31st Infantry augmented with a platoon of LRRPs from Echo Company, and they were on there way to an old French plantation in advance of an artillery unit that was going to set up a fire support base. They were humping in so they could survey and sweep the surrounding area and check out a couple of villages that are suppose to be abandon.

"This whole area is suppose to abandon, and we walked head long into what I estimate to be an entire Viet Cong Regiment. All of a sudden they were everywhere in front of us, behind us, I mean right on top of us just like that."

Flores went on to tell me that once they had the plantation secured the engineers were going to be air lifted in to start building the fire base. There was only two other officers left that weren't wounded or dead and one of them is a brand new Second Lieutenant that has only been in-country a week, and his Platoon Sergeant was one of the first ones killed. The other officer is the Platoon Leader with the LRRP platoon which is cut off somewhere in front of them.

"I've been trying to get him on the radio, but no joy. The last time I heard him was when he talked to the Captain, right after they made contact about fifty meters off our point."

The rain also brought with it a slow down in the fighting and gave the Lieutenant a chance to pull his people in and consolidate his position.

"I've got thirteen plus wounded here. We've been trying to get Dust Offs in for over an hour, the bird you were on was the only thing we've seen, other than some Skyraiders that showed up about twenty minutes ago, just as we were about to be overrun."

"Lieutenant, I've got Echo two six on the radio." Said the radio operator as he handed the Lieutenant the handset.

"Echo two six, this is Bravo six, what's your situation?"

"Two dead and four wounded, making our way back to your location."

"Roger Echo two six, I'll notify Maxwell you're coming in. Bravo six out." "Sanders, get up front and tell Sergeant Maxwell that Echo two is coming in."

"I guess with this rain, you can forget about any air support. What about artillery support?"

"Too far out, we have mortars but I had to wait until we got consolidated and made contact with Echo two, so we didn't plaster them. If you want to help out, Lt. Greenberg is on the left flank, they got hit pretty hard and he can use another man."

"What about a weapon?"

"Weapons and ammo, we have plenty of, just see the Medics."

This was more than just rain, we found ourselves in the middle of a monsoon. It turned the day into dark and we were crawling around in mud, feeling our way, as much as barely being able to see where we were going. The Medics were only about fifteen meters behind us but it took me what seemed like five minutes to get there. The attack had virtually stopped with the rain, only the occasional shot now and then could be heard over the driving rain.

The wounded that were still able to move were being patched up, as well as possible under the circumstances, and sent back to their squads or to the improvised CP, which was not much more than a lean-to made out of ponchos. The Medics were having a hard time trying to keep the more seriously wounded up out of the mud. They had tied the dead together to keep them from floating away, and were pulling the wounded up on top of the bodies to help with the mud and covered them with ponchos.

"Murphy, Murphy." I called in a voice just above a whisper.

"Over here." Came the reply, and I found Murphy, ass deep in mud and covered with a poncho. One of the Medics had stitched up the gash in his leg and bandaged it.

"Can you walk?"

"Not in this shit, but I can crawl." Murphy said and I could see he already had a M16 he was using to prop the poncho up.

I got a M16 off the pile of weapons that the Medics had stacked up. I then stuffed my jungle fatigues pockets with about eight loaded magazines. Murphy and I set off to find Lt. Greenberg on the left flank. A couple of minutes into the crawl, parachute flares started popping off all around the perimeter. With the light of the flares we found our way to the flank. I don't know where

Greenberg was, but the guy in charge was a Staff Sergeant named Washington.

"Who are you guys?" Washington asked.

"Whitley and Murphy, we were on the Huey that crashed." I said then continued. "We're suppose to give Lt. Greenberg a hand."

"Don't worry about the Lieutenant, that's him over there underneath that poncho that's doing all the shaking."

"What's all the flares for, won't they give our position away?" Murphy asked.

"Hell man, don't you think Charlie knows where we are by now. They're for the bombers so they don't dump on us."

"Bombers?" I asked.

"Yeah, the Army can't get to us in this rain, but the Air Force said, *Can Do.*"

More illumination flares started popping all around the perimeter, then three green star clusters went off right in the center where the CP is. We couldn't hear the aircraft in the driving rain, much less see them. Then came the explosions all around us, every time I thought they were about to stop, they would start again. Three runs in all, it seemed like they were right on top of us, but they were seventy-five to a hundred meters out. Close enough that we could feel the concussions and the rain was now filled with clumps of mud and vegetation.

It was a long wet miserable night and those who got some sleep, even if it was only a wink or two, were a lot better off then the rest of us. After the bombing, their mortars stop and even the occasional small arms fire had ceased. The rain finally slacked off then drizzled out completely about 0400 hours.

As daylight slowly came creeping up on the horizon, we found ourselves on the only high ground around. Calling it high ground is kind of misleading, we were only on a slight rise in the surrounding landscape and still ankle deep in mud. It appeared we were on a small mud island in the middle of a vast lake, with tuffs of the tall grass only making sparse appearances here and there. At about 0700 hours we were over flown by a flight of four Cobra gun ships, followed shortly by five Hueys including three Slicks and two Hogs (Huey gun ships). The Cobras continued on and engaged the remaining Viet Cong force that had attacked us and who were also trapped in the water.

While the Hogs circled our position to provide security, the Slicks came in one at a time and hovered just above the mud and allowed us to load up our wounded. With all the wounded on board, including Murphy, we loaded our twelve dead on the last one.

During the night an ARVN armored unit had tried to make it to our location, but had been stopped about three miles to our south by the rain. The rest of us were left to slug through the water and mud, sometimes waist deep, to try and meet up with them. Before we left, all the weapons and equipment that we couldn't carry were piled up and blown with C4.

It took the forty-two of us still standing about four and a half hours to cover the three miles to the ARVN unit. It started raining again just as we arrived and we were all exhausted and wanted time to remove the leaches that covered our bodies, but the ARVN Commander was nervous and didn't want to remain in the area long enough for us to clean up. So we loaded up inside and on top of the armored personnel carriers and headed for the ARVN base camp at the old French fort on the edge of the Indigo Jungle.

When we arrived we wanted to hit the field showers that were set up, but we had to be checked-out by the Medics first. The Medics removed the leaches and checked our feet. I was chafed raw and bleeding from the crotch to my knees on the inside of both legs and several blisters on both feet that had to be lanced. During the shower I washed my fatigues and web gear and cleaned the mud out of my 45 and the M16 I had picked up. After the shower and a stop at the weapons cleaning table, wearing nothing but a towel rapped around my waist, I hit the unit supply room and exchanged my uniform and boots for a new set. I made a mistake by turning in the M16 that I had picked up after the crash, but I wouldn't realize that until later.

After I got something to eat, I found an empty bunk and got about three hours of sleep then I got up and started looking for a ride home.

I got a ride on a Huey going to Dong Tam then a ride on a C130 going to Bear Cat.

When I arrived at Bear Cat I used the phone at the airfield to call the office. Big M answered the phone and I asked him if Caffey could come and pick me up.

"Caffey left yesterday, where have you been, the Captain was about to list you missing with the Company?"

"It's a long story. What about that ride?"

"Yeah, hang on. Let me tell the Captain you are OK, and I'll come and pick you up."

On the ride to the office, Big M filled me in on Tran and Feldman who were both in the field hospital. Feldman was going to be OK, but Tran had severe 2d and 3d degree burns over his hands, arms and face. I told Big M about Tran getting into the burning M113 to get to the machine gun, and he told me to make sure I put that in my after action report.

When we got back to the office, the Captain was on his way out.

"Well, glad to see you're still with us Sergeant Whitley."

"Yeah, me too, sir. I wasn't sure I was going to make it back for a while."

"Write it up and I'll read it when I get back from MACV." The Captain said as he threw his bag into a jeep and headed out.

I asked Lt Parrish what was going on, and he said that some replacement personnel that were scheduled in had been cancelled and the Captain was going to MACV to find out what the deal is.

I finished up my after action report and gave it to Parrish to read. He looked it over and told me to take the rest of the day off.

The next morning the Captain still wasn't back. Parrish said he was going to the hospital to see Tran and I asked if I could go with him. We didn't get in to see Tran because they had him in a *clean room,* because of his burns We did find Feldman and he was in the middle of one of his stories telling everyone who would listen how he killed fifty Cong and saved the day with his heroics. I asked about Murphy, but they said he must be at another hospital.

The Captain was back when we returned and had some bad news for all of us, but especially for me. The unit is moving to II Corps. The Captain and Parrish are the only ones going. Their new mission will be coordinating intelligence operations for the Field Force. Big M is going to Saigon to work at VE-AD and the MPs are going back to there parent unit. The two remaining contact teams are being dissolved and the 525th Military Intelligence Group has determined that I am not qualified to hold my 97C, Intelligence Area Analyst MOS. Wow! It took some real intelligence work to figure that one out, especially since they sent me to Vietnam instead of the school, like they were suppose to. Anyway, I am being assigned to the 1st Air Cavalry Division and I have four days to pack my gear and report in.

While clearing the Company I was given a ration of crap from the Supply Scrgeant because I didn't have my M16 to turn-in. I explained that I lost it in a helicopter crash, but he didn't believe me, and said I needed verification signed by an officer. In the mean time he would initiate a "statement of charges", which means unless I can prove the weapon was a "combat loss", I would be paying for it and could be subject to charges under the Uniform Code of Military Justice. Of course, I didn't believe it would go that far, I just get flustered with the way the Army does things sometimes. There's only one way to do things in the Army and that's the *Army Way*. I went back to the office to see if Captain Sullivan would write me a letter, but he was wrapped up in problems of his own and said the only thing he had to go by was my after action report and he couldn't release that because it was classified.

"What I will do is get a message off to Lieutenant Flores with the 6th of the 31st Infantry Battalion, and to the 555th Aviation to get confirmation about your presents there and the helicopter crash. It's not that I don't believe you, you just have to cross all the t's and dot all the i's to satisfy the Army bean counters."

"Yes Sir, I understand."

"Look, Sergeant Whitley, you'll be gone before this stuff gets back, but I'll make sure it gets taken care of."

"Thank you, Sir. Well I better be getting back to clearing this place." I said and saluted the Captain then turned to leave when the Captain called me back.

"Whitley."

"Yes Sir."

"According to this report you made, you were in some scary shit out there. Anyway, I've got to go back to Saigon for a couple of days tomorrow and may not make it back before you leave, but you will be hearing from me. Good luck and keep your ass down."

"Yes Sir, that thought had crossed my mind."

CHAPTER 7

Airmoble

Well I cleared Bear Cat and would be on my way to Camp Evans to join the 1st Air Cavalry Division in the morning with a "statement of charges" for a M16 rifle and a "Line of Duty" investigation hanging over my head. My MOS according to my orders was back to being a 71L, Administrative NCO.

The rain was just stopping and it was wet and cold as I waited on the tarmac, with all my earthly positions packed into a single duffle bag, waiting, just waiting for the C130 that would take me up north. The plane was packed with Sky Troopers from the 1st Cav, several personnel from a medical unit, some Air Force guys, and Marines, all going to Camp Evans. If I hadn't been in the shit before, I was headed for it now, and it's strange the things you think about in times like this, it is the 31st of March, 1968, my brother David's birthday, and I wondered what he and my sisters, back in Kentucky would be doing today.

We landed at Camp Evans and the sun was well into burning the chill out of the air. I got directions to the Personnel Office, threw my duffle bag over my shoulder and headed out. Well I found the office I needed, but things were in an uproar, kind of like an organized chaos. I finally got the attention of a Sergeant and he sent me to a Lieutenant, one of the assistant Personnel Officers. The Lieutenant took a copy of my orders and disappeared into the crowd of soldiers. When he returned, he said.

"I don't have anything on you Sergeant Whitley, normally we would keep you with us for a while, but the Major says the 3d Brigade is screaming for replacements so that's where you are headed." The Lieutenant then continued. "Specialist Daniels, drive Sergeant Whitley over to 3d Brigade Headquarters."

When we got into the jeep, I asked Daniels if things were always so hectic.

"Not really, we have a big operation starting tomorrow and have a lot of personnel transferring in."

"What kind of operation?" I asked.

"Operation Pegasus, it seems the Marines have their ass in a jam in Khe Sanh, and we're going in to save their bacon."

Daniels dropped me off at Brigade Headquarters and I made my way to the S1, Personnel Office. The officer there told me that all Staff Sergeants and above check-in with the Brigade Sergeant Major first and directed me down the hall. I finally caught up to the Sergeant Major in the S3, Operations, office. The Sergeant Major looked at my orders and 201 file for a few moments, then finally spoke to me.

"It says here that you lost your weapon in combat. What's a clerk doing in combat?"

"I was in a helicopter crash in the Plain of Reeds when I lost my M16."

"And what the hell were you doing in a helicopter in the Plain of Reeds? Sit down Whitley, I've got to hear this, I haven't had my ration of bull shit yet today."

So I briefly related the events that lead up to the crash and the march back to the old French Fort on the edge of the Indigo Jungle.

"Door gunner. Well good, I don't have any jobs for clerks right now, but I have plenty of jobs for door gunners with Operation Pegasus starting tomorrow, so get your ass over to the 2d of the 7th, and tell them I said you are a door gunner."

When I got to the 2d Battalion and reported in, I was sent to see the Supply Sergeant where I drew a steel pot, flak-jacket, field gear, and a M16 with ammo.

"7th Cavalry, wasn't that General Custer's unit at the Little Big Horn?" I asked half kidding.

"That's right Sarg, only they won't be shooting arrows and throwing spears at you tomorrow. What made you volunteer to be a door gunner?"

"I think the Brigade Sergeant Major volunteered me."

"Yeah, I know what you mean. They've got half the clerks and cooks in the Battalion assigned to door gunner duty. They even *volunteered* my assistant."

I got my other pair of boots, extra socks and a set of fatigues out, rolled them and put them in my pack and left my duffle bag with the Supply Sergeant and asked directions to the mess hall.

"Out the door, turn right, about four buildings down. You can't miss it."

"Thanks Sergeant, and one more thing. What's this *Gary Owen* I see and hear everywhere?"

"Gary Owen. It's the 7th Cavalry motto, they use it like a greeting or an affirmative response, just tradition."

"Well, Gary Owen Sergeant."

At chow a Sergeant First Class in a flight suit came in and yelled for all the new door gunners to meet him behind the mess hall at 1800 hours. At he meeting there was eleven of us, there was two cooks, the rest were clerks from various offices at Battalion and Brigade Headquarters. The one thing we all had in common was that everyone had at least fired a M60 machinegun. We were given the time table. Wakeup - 0330 hours, Breakfast - 0400 hours, Equipment check - 0445 hours,

Assembly area for final briefing - 0515 hours, Zero hour and take off - 0600 hours. The Sergeant told us to all bunk in building 22 at the airfield tonight.

I didn't think I would be able to sleep, but I was wrong. After talking with another Staff Sergeant from Battalion Operations, who had volunteered to be a door gunner for this mission, who said this was going to be the biggest air lift since the 1st Cav has been in Vietnam, I fell fast asleep. I mean dead to the world. The next thing I knew some one was yelling, "It's time to get up, let's move it!"

At the assembly area it was unusually foggy, you could barely see the aircraft on the tarmac. After the briefing I hooked up with the Crew Chief on the bird I was assigned to, and I'm glad he knew where it was parked among all the choppers on the field, because I would have never found it in the fog.

After the Crew Chief made his flight engineer checks, we just sat back and waited. At 0600 hours we were still waiting, the fog wasn't going anywhere, you couldn't see more than ten feet in front of yourself. Well after daylight we were still waiting, the Crew Chief told me to stay with the bird and he went to go see what was going on. With the sun starting to burn some of the fog off, I was amazed at how many helicopters I could see and I could only see what was parked closest to us.

"Get some sleep if you can, it's going to be at least two or three more hours before we can get out of here. They don't want to take any chances with so many choppers taking off at once" The crew chief told me, and I couldn't hold off any longer so I asked.

"Sergeant Knife, what kind of name is that?"

"It's actually Big Elk Broken Knife, well that is the translation from Crow. When I joined the Army they shortened it to just Knife, but everybody just calls me Chief."

"Do you like that?"

"What?" He asked.

"People calling you Chief."

"Not at first, but now I just consider it White Mans ignorance. Anyway, my friends call me Amos."

"OK, Amos. Don't start without me." I said and laughed as I laid my flack jacket down and used it as a pillow to rest my head on. It was a nervous laugh, as I was wound up so tight in my gut, that I was about to explode, and the waiting and waiting wasn't helping any. If we could just get started, I thought, the nervousness would fade into excitement.

At 1230 hours the pilot, a Warrant Officer Benson, showed up and he and Sergeant Knife started doing the pre-flight.

Finally, at 1315 hours, seven hours past our take off time, I heard someone on a loud speaker yelling. "Gary Owen, boots and saddles. Then someone else yelling. "Second Battalion, saddle up, let's move it."

By this time I could see the mass of helicopters on the field. There was at least eight big Chinooks, thirty, forty plus Hueys, sixteen Cobra gunship's that I could see, and a hand full LOH's, Light Observation Helicopters for Command and Control and Field Artillery observation.

The first to take off were the Cobras, LOH's and two of the Chinooks, which carried the only Marines we had with us. Their mission was to secure the two Landing Zones, LZ Mike and LZ Cates while we put boots on the ground. Finally in the air, the Hueys carried Alpha Company, 2d of the 7th Cav, and two of the other Chinooks carried artillery.

We dropped off Alpha Company in the first wave, and by the time we got back with Charlie Company the battle was underway. Even though the Air Force bombers had taken out most of the North Vietnamese anti-aircraft guns the night before we were still under continuous fire in and out of both Landing Zones. LZ Mike was the worst, we took several hits to the helicopter both flying in and out for the first five turn-a-rounds. We got a brief break while we re-fueled and got more ammo for the M60. We had actually leapfrogged over a North Vietnamese battalion going into LZ Mike, so I had plenty targets of opportunity both in and out of the Landing Zones. The pilot made it look easy dodging the RPGs and B40 rockets being fired at us. The smoke trails were like an arrow in the sky showing me exactly where to fire. After we refueled and we continued moving troops unto the battle zone, we had to detour around the hot area, because the Air Force had jets in the area laying waist to the North Vietnamese unit we had jumped over. We continued taking troops in and bringing wounded out until about 1830 hours, by then the air space was secure enough for the Dust-off crews to take over bringing the wounded out.

My God, Airmobile. On April the first, 1968 the 1st Air Cavalry Division kicked off Operation Pegasus, a massive air assault to break the siege at Khe Sanh. Leading the way was Alpha and Charlie Companies of the 2d Battalion of the 7th Cavalry, followed by the rest of the battalion, then the rest of 3d Brigade. Within two days 5 more LZs were secured and the rest of the Division with First and Second Brigades were engaged. AIRMOBILE. That word will forever have a special meaning for me. In the course of about 5 and 1/2 hours an entire combat brigade including field artillery and support units was loaded and delivered to within two miles of the besieged base at Khe Sanh and immediately engaged the enemy army holding siege to the base.

Prior to today 3500 Marines, 2100 ARVN Rangers and other personnel at Khe Sanh have endured weeks of a literal hell on earth with almost constant barrage of mortars, field artillery and rockets. All the time fending off periodic attacks on the perimeter. They held on, with the airfield now destroyed beyond use and air supply by helicopter becoming harder and harder. On the perimeter holding the line are a couple of young Marines from Kentucky, Sergeants Larry T. Brady and Ronald B. Mudd, who in a later life would become brothers-in-law, but at this time their brotherhood has already been forged in blood along with the other Marines at Khe Sanh.

Artillery duels ensued along with heavy, bloody, sometimes hand to hand ground combat. After the airlift the extra door gunners were released back to their regular jobs, and I was assigned to Headquarters, 2d of the 7th Cavalry in S3 Operations to replace the Air Ops NCO that had been killed in the first two days of Pegasus. By the end of the 3d day our units had broken the back of the NVA Artillery and silenced their 130mm cannons.

With the entire 1st Air Cavalry engaged, the outcome was inevitable. The NVA were leaving there dead as well as massive amounts of equipment, arms and ammunition as they retreated from the battlefield. At about 0800 hours April 8, 1968 PFC Juan Fordoni, from Puerto Rico, was the first Sky Trooper to make contact as he clasped hands over the barbed wire with a Marine Lance Corporal. Soon to follow were signs reading "Under New Management, complements of the 1st Air Cavalry Division."

I was not long for my job in the Battalion S3, I was given verbal orders to pack my gear and report to the Division Sergeant Major. I thought that the Army had finally seen the error of its ways assigning a sharp fellow like me to a Battalion when I should be assigned to Division Headquarters. Well, I was wrong of course. The Division Sergeant Major advised me that the "Statement of Charges" for the loss of a M16 rifle had been resolved and was certified to be a "combat loss" and I wouldn't have to pay for it, but I should be more careful in the future. "Well thank you very much, Uncle Sam." He also informed me that I was being reassigned to MACV Headquarters in Saigon. So here I go again back to MACV. I wish the Army would make up it's mind.

CHAPTER 8

High Expectations
(usually lead to disappointment)

After my orders arrived the trip down south was uneventful except for the C130 we were waiting for, blowing a tire on landing and skidding off the runway. After about an hour of the scheduled passengers sitting on the tarmac in the sun cooking like lobsters until the rain started, then we just steamed. The powers that be finally came up with a couple of C47s to cram all of us into and off we went. At the airfield there were air conditioned busses headed to Camp Alpha for the guys going back to the states and trucks for the rest of us. I talked my way on to one of the Camp Alpha busses. An air conditioned bus sure sounded better then riding in the back of a truck in the heat. I figured I could catch a ride to MACV from

Camp Alpha. There was a shuttle bus going to the units in the Saigon area leaving every hour, so I decided to take a break and hit the NCO Club for a steak and backed potato before I headed out. I mean, who knows where I'm going to end up spending the night, I might as well get a good meal in me while I can.

After arriving at MACV Headquarters the Duty Officer told me to grab a bunk at the transit barracks and report back the next day. After reporting in, I was told I was being assigned to an outfit called CORDS, (Civil Operations and Revolutionary Development Support Agency), now that's a mouth full. I arrived at CORDS Operational Headquarters, which looked like it was being run by civilians, very few uniforms in sight. Finally I saw a Major in uniform that looked like he worked there and asked him where I report in.

"Are you sure you have the right place, Sergeant?" The way he asked made me think that maybe I was in the wrong place. He then asked for a copy of my orders.

After reading my orders he started to give me directions back to MACV Headquarters.

"Yes sir, I have already been to MACV and was told that I am being assigned to CORDS."

"Well this is the headquarters. Follow me and I'll show you where Personnel and Finance is located. Maybe they know something."

"Yes sir." I replied as I followed him down a hallway, out a door, across a small courtyard and into another building.

"This is it." The Major said and followed with. "Good luck."

I finally found someone that would stop working long enough to ask me what I was doing there. After another 10 minutes of the old army run-a-round, a Warrant Officer got a copy of my orders and went to make a phone call. When he returned, The Officer told me that I was correct, I am being assigned to CORDS, but my duty station will be with VE-AD. I told him I was familiar with VE-AD, and he said he would get someone to drive me to the compound.

At the VD-AD compound I went directly to Colonel Augden's office and was going to knock on the door, when it opened. The Vietnamese lady that was leaving smiled and before I could say anything, I heard Colonel Augden's voice.

"Whitley, come in here. Close the door and have a seat. Have you got a cigarette?" "Never mind." He said as he saw the pack of Pall Malls come out of my pocket.

I replied in the affirmative and did as I was told, only pausing long enough to salute.

"Sorry about the runaround, but we are pulling men from several different agencies for the Phoenix Program, that's where you will be working."

"What is Phoenix, exactly, sir?"

"The Phoenix Program is divided into three parts." Just then a knock at the door. "That should be Jack Roark." The Colonel said as the door opened and Roark stuck his head in, then entered.

"Sorry I was delayed, I had to wait for a telex from Washington." Roark said as he entered the room. "It concerns Phoenix." Roark handed the paper to Augden.

After reading the paper, the Colonel looked up and said. "Well, I see Johnson finally got off his ass and signed the Presidential directive for Sword. That's the third part of Phoenix that I was getting ready to tell you about, but I'll let Jack do it."

"As you may, or may not know, Operation Phoenix, also known as the Phoenix Program has been under way for about two months. At least the first two parts of it. HEARTS, building schools, health clinics and food programs in remote villages. HANDS, to supplement the Special Forces training of villagers, the CIA has implemented a plan to train and arm three 600 man militias, one in each Corps area. These militias will be self contained, including artillery, air and logistical support. They will operate independently of the ARVN Army under a centralized CIA command."

"Let me interject something here." Augden said then continued. "Almost at once, it became clear that certain elements of the Vietnamese government from the Palace right down to some District and Village chiefs, including some Commanders in the ARVN Army opposed Phoenix."

"A lot more than opposed." Roark continued and handed Augden a Salem in response to the Colonel's two fingered gesture. "In some cases, overtly conspiring against operations to include giving intelligence to the

North. Some of these individuals have been suspected of being sympathizers and communist agents."

"Hence, the third part of Phoenix, that Johnson has finally given his approval of." Augden interjected again, as Roark walked over to the book case and pulled open two doors that reveled a small bar.

Roark poured himself a scotch and tilted the bottle toward Augden, who nodded in the affirmative. "What about you, Whitley?" Roark asked, but I just shuck my head, no.

Roark handed the Colonel his drink, shut the doors to the bar and continued talking. "Right, the third part, SWORD. We are going to eliminate the opposition to Phoenix. By that I mean the people on the list will have their opposition terminated permanently." "Do you understand what I'm saying?" Roark directed his question toward me.

"Yes Sir, terminated permanently." I said wondering what my part in all this would be. I didn't have to wonder long.

Roark finished his drink then continued talking. "There are three "K" teams ready to go on Sword, although there are some Special Forces operators, most of the men are mercenaries. You will coordinate the team in the delta, call sign Kitchen Three. They will receive their targets, logistical support and pay from you. You will be their only contact with us. At no time will you use either Colonel Augden's or my name, you will refer to us only as Chef. Do you understand?"

"So far, Sir, but I will have some questions." I said feeling like a man whose death sentence had just been announced in court.

"Well, hold your questions for later, there will be time for that." Augden said then Roark continued.

"Look Sergeant Whitley, it's not like you will be in combat. Like I said, your job will be to coordinate, facilitate and verify that the missions are conducted. After each mission you will report directly to me at the Embassy to brief me and pick up their pay and next target. Each time you will return any target information you were given back to me. You will keep nothing in writing or discuss your job with anyone except me or Colonel Augden. Before your questions, Colonel Augden has more information for you."

"Take some time off, you are due for a 3 day in-country R&R. You can go to Vung Tau, China Beach or stay right here in Saigon at Camp Alpha. When you get back, I'll have Sky Hook travel orders for you that will allow you to request air craft or fly anywhere in-country on a "Priority Alpha" basis. I'll also have new identification for you, identifying you as a VE-AD civilian employee. The Sword part of Phoenix is strictly a non-military operation. Now, do you have any questions?"

"Yes Sir. Do I have a choice?"

"Look Sergeant, Jack has recommended you very strongly for this job. I trust Jack and he trust you to carry out this mission and keep your mouth shut. If he had any doubts about you being able to do this job, you wouldn't be going. As far as you having a choice, of course you have a choice. There are a lot of unsafe places here in Vietnam, and you have a lot of time left to go, so where would you rather be, a safe job like this with people looking out for you, or, stuck out in some rice paddy with people shooting at you?"

Colonel Augden didn't wait for an answer, and really there was no need to, the choice was obvious. The Colonel sent me down the hall to the Ops room to get my R&R orders typed up and have some photos taken. I saw Big M, he was working in operations at VE-AD now, and we talked briefly about how Captain Sullivan and Lt. Parrish were making out in their new assignment up north. Bill said that he sees Sullivan on a regular basis, when he makes duty trips to Saigon.

I decided to stay in Saigon as Camp Alpha had every thing I needed except a beach. There was a swimming pool, NCO club, USO club and a snack bar and PX. Right outside the gate was Madam Xu's Steam Bath, one of the local boom boom palaces.

So for three days, I ate a lot and drank a lot. In fact did everything a lot including swimming in the late afternoon and dozing off in the big overstuffed easy chair listening to the pounding of the rain on the air conditioner at the USO club in the mornings. I tried not to think too much of my upcoming job, and for the most part I was successful. Three days doesn't sound like a long time, but in Vietnam, three days could be a lifetime. The torrential rains seemed to confine themselves to the morning hours and it was raining when the jeep came to take me back to the VE-AD compound.

When I got to Colonel Augden's office, there was some small talk about my R&R, but he soon got down to business. I turned over my ID Card and dog tags as requested and received my new ID as a civilian employee of VE-AD and Sky Hook travel authorization.

I noticed that the travel orders were valid for a period of 6 months, and asked. "Will the operation last for 6 months, like it says on the orders?"

"No. Not your part of it. Two maybe three months at the most, then you can have your choice of assignments." Augden paused for a moment and just looked at me. Then with kind of a half laugh he asked. "Does that meet with your approval?"

He didn't need my approval, he was just trying to lift the air in the room. I guess my fear and apprehension were showing.

"Don't worry Sergeant. The job is mostly a lot of running back and forth. You're actually just a messenger, the mission plans will be worked up by the team and their leader, Lieutenant Forette."

"I thought you said these guys are mercenaries."

"They are. Jack told me that Forette and Muesell are left over Frenchmen, ex-legionnaires' that stayed in Vietnam after the French left. Forette married into an old rubber plantation family. His wife, Cia Hanh, is the only daughter and heir, but with the war the plantation has fallen on hard times. That's when he was recruited by my predecessor for intelligence gathering. Ex Lt. Forette was approached by his handler at the time, to see if he would be interested in this kind of work. We have never met the man, but here is a picture of him. Look at it then let me have it back for the file." Augden said as he handed me the old picture of two men standing in front of an artillery piece.

I looked at the photograph that was starting to yellow and asked. "Which one is Forette?"

"The younger man on the left." He said pointing with the cigarette he was smoking.

"And the other one is Muesell?" I asked.

"No. The other man is Colonel Piroth. He was the artillery commander at Dien Bien Phu and blamed himself for the fix the French found themselves in. General Giap, the same General Vo Nguyen Giap that we are still fighting today, had surrounded the French and captured three of Piroth's fire bases located on the surrounding hills. Colonel Piroth found himself "completely dishonored", his words supposedly, and committed suicide shortly after this picture was taken by blowing himself up with a grenade. That's when the French decided to get the hell out of Vietnam."

"Too bad we didn't learn anything from the French." I said without thinking and immediately wished I had kept my mouth shut. I handed the photograph back to Colonel Augden.

"Look Sergeant Whitley, we're going to win this war."

"Yes Sir. I only meant that the French really screwed it up."

"OK Sergeant. You're suppose to be a civilian now, so get over to the supply room, it's the building with the Conex containers beside it, get geared up, and report to Roark at the Embassy."

I stood up, saluted, and headed to the supply room. The Colonel must have called because the guy was waiting for me. I picked up 2 pair of black jungle fatigues with no patches on them and signed for a 45 auto with two clips and a fifty round box of ammunition. A pistol belt with holster, canteen, poncho and poncho liner was the extent of the web gear.

"You look to be the same size as Cal Mason." He said as he placed a B4 bag on the counter. "Take this, it's getting in the way around here."

"What happened to Mason?" I asked as I looked inside the bag.

"Don't know. A guy from the Embassy came by and collected his personal effects, and left this stuff behind. So I doubt if he's going to come back looking for it."

There wasn't much of any value inside the bag, a couple of civilian shirts, some other clothes, playing cards and a few magazines. I took off my Staff Sergeant collar pins, threw them inside the bag along with the gear I just received, except for the pistol belt and weapon which I put on. I clipped my VE-AD ID card on to my shirt pocket, and put the Defense Department civilian employee ID card in my wallet. I didn't bother to change shirts, the fatigues I had on were DX (direct exchange) and didn't have any unit patches, name tag or US Army on them. I grabbed the bag along with my duffel and headed back out the door and put them in the back of the jeep that was waiting for me.

"We're going to stop by the hotel, that's where most of the CORDS, VE-AD, Embassy personnel and some of the correspondents are quartered." The driver paused for a moment while the guards opened the gate. "I'm Charlie, Charlie Gibson, by the way. I work at the Embassy, down the hall from Jack. You'll be bunking in with me." "If that's all right with you?"

"Yeah, sure Charlie, the name is Ron Whitley, but you can just call me Whitley. But, I probably won't be spending much time there. I'm going to be working in the field."

"I know, Jack told me." Charlie said.

"What else did Jack tell you?"

"Not much. Just, not to ask you what you will be doing, but, that's pretty standard for Jack."

"How long have you known Jack?"

"Well, I got here about two months ago, and I just know him from the Embassy." "How about you, known Jack, I mean?"

"I met him last year at the Embassy in Germany, then ran into him over here."

"I bet you're army or ex-army, you've got that look."

"Yeah, something like that." I said.

"I know. I talk too much."

There was no more conversation until we pulled into the hotel. Charlie was occupied with his driving through the streets of Saigon, I don't think he missed many of the mud puddles on the way. The hotel was nice, there was a bar and restaurant with several people milling around, and the room upstairs had a window air conditioner that was running full blast. I sorted out my duffle bag threw some more stuff in the B4 bag and put the duffle in the closet. I didn't bother putting anything in drawers.

"Are you ready?" Charlie asked.

"Ready as I'm ever going to be." I said as I picked up my B4 bag and we headed back downstairs to the vehicle.

At the Embassy I cleared my weapon at the security check point, then went inside and down the hall to Jack Roark's office. I knocked on the door then tried the door knob and opened the door. Jack was standing by the door putting on the jacket to his cheap seersucker suit.

"Whitley. You're here. Good, drop your bag and come on and I'll buy you lunch."

I deposited my bag in the chair across from his desk and followed him back out the door. After Jack locked the door we went down to the Embassy cafeteria. There was no talking about the operation while we were eating, just chitchat about Vietnam in general. Jack said he found a real good restaurant that was close to the Embassy and that he would take me there the next time I came up. I thought at this point at least he thinks I will be coming back.

Back in the office, I removed my bag from the chair and sat down to read the file Jack had taken out of his safe.

"As you can see your first target is Fang Dien Nguyen, the Chief of Police of Viet Can Province."

"And we're sure he's one of the bad guys. I mean, there's no chance of a mistake."

"Look, these targets have been scrutinized to death. If there was any doubt at all, they wouldn't be on the list. So let's just assume that the people responsible know what they're doing."

"I was just thinking out loud, that's all." I said, resisting the urge to make a comment about the "Peter Principle" and the people in charge. The file also contained Fang's usual routine and some surveillance notes. Also included in the file was personal information and photographs.

"You are going to be operating out of Forette's in-laws rubber plantation east of the Cua Soir river close to Phu Thanh. You should be secure there, the Plantation manager makes payoffs to the local, shall we say, political organization."

"You mean the Viet Cong. Forette's plantation is supporting the VC?" I asked, not believing what I was hearing.

"Only as a business decision made out of necessity. Things get a little confusing sometimes in this business, but it does give us a good place to operate out of."

I finished reading the file, then looked up at Roark and asked. "What's next?"

"Next. Next you grab your bag and head out. Across from the Embassy there will be a black taxi with red lettering that says Duc Phan Taxi. Mr. Duc works for us and will take you across the river to the Foo Hanh rubber plantation."

"Forette?"

"Right. That's where you'll find Forette. You let him plan the operation, but you have final approval. If you need anything special, you let me know in person and I'll get it for you. When you are ready to go, have Forette call this number, it is a local flower shop and ask if his order is ready. They will either say yes or no, that's your final go or no go on the operation." "Understand?"

"Got it." I said as I got up to leave.

"Oh, and Whitley, a certain amount of collateral damage is to be expected, but keep it under control."

I didn't say anything else as I left. I just turned back briefly to look at him in acknowledgement.

CHAPTER 9

The Plantation

The taxi ride didn't take as long as expected. Actually, I didn't know what to expect, but was surprised to find out we were only about 40 minutes outside of Saigon when we arrived at the Plantation. The taxi stopped at an iron gate that was manned by Vietnamese workers. I grabbed my bag from the taxi and the workers opened the gate for me with out questions. It was a beautiful walk down the tree lined drive to the main Plantation house. I passed several paths leading off the main drive. One of the paths went to what appeared to be a large storage building and another lead to a large cluster of smaller buildings, probably worker houses, I thought to my self.

The main house was a faded chalky looking white and there was a large covered porch that extended across the entire front of the house and down the sides. The plantation house must have been an impressive sight in its time, but now appeared to be a little run down. I was greeted at the main entrance by a beautiful Vietnamese woman who looked to be in her early thirties.

"This way please." She said in English but with a heavy French accent and I followed her into the large room with exceptionally high ceilings and beautifully appointed mahogany furniture. She clapped her hands and an older Vietnamese man appeared wearing black slacks and a white short sleeved servants jacket. He took my bag and we followed him across the room and down a hall on the left. We stopped briefly at one of the bedrooms. The older man took my bag into the room after I retrieved the large envelope that was in the side zipper compartment. We continued on to the end of the hall to a large office with a mixture of old, but still elegant, sofas, chairs, tables and more modern desks, file and chart cabinets and telephones. The room seemed odd in appearance at first, especially with all the furniture and a table full of radios and communication gear in one corner and the expensive but well worn hard wood floors.

"Please, make yourself comfortable. Would you like something cold to drink." She said as she motioned for me to set on one of the sofas." She clapped her hands again, and the little man come into the room. She spoke to him in Vietnamese then addressed me again. "Alain will be with you shortly." She followed the servant out of the room.

I was starting to get a little fidgety and stood up and starting to pace when another servant, a young girl this time, carrying a tray with a pitcher of what looked like lemonade and some glasses, entered the room. She poured a glass for me and I sat back down. I could hear Vietnamese voices and a lot of movement out side the window. I went to the window and it appeared to be a hand full of workers coming in for the day. I could also hear voices in the house now, and suspected it wouldn't be long before I met Alain Forette.

The footsteps echoing on the wood floor coming down the hall preceded the arrival of two men, neither of them was Forette.

"Hello, I'm Delbert Foo, the plantation manager. I bet you didn't expect to see another American here. Well half American anyway." The short, rather rotund, Asian man said.

"Hello, Mister Foo. Whitley here." I said as I stood to shake his hand.

"*Just* Whitley. Well, we have another one, I see."

"Excuse me?" I said, not understanding what he meant.

"Oh, the quiet Frenchman at the desk, he's *just* Muesell. You can call me Dell by the way, everyone else does."

Muesell nodded in my direction then opened the bottom drawer of the desk and pulled out a bottle of cognac and poured himself about three fingers into one of the glasses from the tray setting on the desk. Dell also poured himself a lemonade and a silence engulfed the room as we all sipped our drinks. More footsteps, this time it was Forette.

He was definitely not what I thought the leader of a group of assassins would look like. Seeing the picture of Forette hadn't offered much. Forette was a short, slender, good looking man with a full head of black hair. He stood about 5' 7" and appeared to be very fit.

"Hello, I'm Alain, and you are the man with the plan." He said as he walked up to me and offered to shake hands.

"Well, I'm the man with the information and you are the man with the plan, or will be." I shook hands and handed him the envelope I was carrying.

"We take care of this later. First we eat, dinner will be in about twenty minutes." Forette said as he took the envelope, and with out opening it, locked it in the top drawer of the desk. "You can meet DeKemp and Borland at dinner, but now we have to clean up."

The men all left the room and I refilled my glass and walked down the hall to my room. I say my room. There were two beds and my bag was sitting on one of them so I sat my glass down and started to unpack. Then I realized that most of the room was occupied so I decided to just leave my things on the bed. There were two doors, one coming in from the hall way and a set of French doors that opened up to a open courtyard in the center of the house. The walk way was lined with flowers and herbs and there was a small vegetable garden at the end where there was a iron gate. It appeared that all the bedrooms opened up onto the courtyard. There were three rooms and the office on the side I was on and directly opposite it looked like another four rooms. I took my lemonade and went outside and sat on a iron bench and smoked a cigarette. I heard movement behind me and looked over my shoulder. It was Muesell standing in the doorway.

"Come. We eat now." He said as he closed the French doors and came outside. I followed him down the path toward the center of the house. There was a large dinning table out side, but we went through another set of doors into the dinning room.

Over a dinner of soup, pork, rice, fresh vegetables and wine, I met the family. Cia Forette, the Vietnamese lady that greeted me when I arrived, presided over the well prepared meal. She commanded the servants with her hand claps and occasional glances. There were three children at the long table, two boys and a little girl. Philip, Cia and Alain's son, was flanked on each side by the children of Delbert Foo and his Vietnamese wife. Muesell who added almost nothing to the dinner conversation, and the two Afrikaners, white South Africans, Brian DeKemp, Sig Borland and myself made up the four single men at the table. The only single woman at the table was Karen DeKemp, Brian's sister.

Brian DeKemp had been the manager of gem mine in Cambodia and Sig Borland was a mining engineer. They, along with Brian's sister had been run out of Cambodia by a new social reform movement calling themselves the Khmer Rouge. Delbert's father had been one of their brokers in Hong Kong so after escaping to Vietnam they ended up here at the plantation. Delbert Foo's father is a Chinese-American business man in Hong Kong who married a Chinese woman and had invested in a rubber plantation in Vietnam that belong to Cia's father, Dien Hanh. After Hanh's death eight years earlier, in an accident on the plantation, Delbert, the number two son, was sent to Vietnam to protect his father's investment and learn the rubber business.

Alain had met and fell in love with Cia Hanh in 1952, while he was a young officer in the Foreign Legion stationed in Vietnam. Cia's father had never accepted Alain until the French pulled out of Vietnam and Alain decided to stay. Cia's father then looked upon Alain Forette as the son he never had and expected him to take over the plantation some day.

A family. A big extended family, not the band of assassin mercenaries Roark had eluded to, but then again, when were things ever as Roark said they would be. At least four of the five were ex-soldiers. Brian and Sig had served together during the Zulu war, and Alain and Muesell were both ex-legionnaires.

English seemed to be the common language at the dinner table. The conversation centered around rubber and plantation affairs and no one broached the subject of my presents at the plantation. I was seated next to Karen DeKemp, she was polite and engaging in conversation, but seemed to have an air of aloofness about her. After coffee and brandy we retired to the office, with the exception of Delbert, who did not join us.

Muesell shut the door as Alain went to the desk to retrieve the envelope I had given him earlier. I sat on one of the sofas and lit a cigarette as the others gathered around Alain Forette and waited for him to say something after going over the file. Finally he passed the file around and one by one they looked over the papers and photographs without saying a word. Finally the silence was broken.

"Well. What do you think? Anybody." Alain asked in general.

"Not so tuff, I think. As long as we can get away with it." Was Borland's input.

"What do you mean, not so tuff. A Policeman. Not just a Policeman, but the Chief of Police." DeKemp said.

"What does that have to do with it? Borland replied, then continued. "Anyone can be killed."

"He's right, you know. Anyone can be killed." Muesell spoke up. "What did you think when we all agreed to do this. That it would be easy."

"That's right. We all agreed to do this because we all need the money." Brian, you need the money to get you and your sister out of here. The same with you Sig, and Muesell needs the money for, shall we say, more whisky and women." Alain was definitely the leader and managed to ease the tension and bring a smile to everyone's face.

"The whisky I agree with, but with my good looks, the women come easy." Muesell said and everyone laughed this time.

"And I need the money to keep things running around here until this damn war is over." Alain said.

"Yes, I understand. We all need the money, but first we need to do some surveillance of our own." DeKemp said.

"Of course Brian, I agree. Muesell will take Xu Tan and go over to Viet Can and check things out for a couple of days. When they get back we will put together a plan. Look, if it's no good, we won't do it."

Oh, the job was going to get done alright. Alain was just trying to reassure Brian DeKemp, who seemed to be the nervous one of the bunch. Xu Tan, as it turns out is a life long member of the plantation family. In fact, the majority of the twenty odd workers were born on the plantation. Mister Tu and his wife are two of the three servants, and the only ones to live in the main house. All the workers live right here on the plantation and Delbert Foo's wife conducts a school for the children and is a trained nurse.

Except for bringing in supplies the plantation is a self contained closed community with a population of about 50 including the wives and children of the workers. In better days the plantation employed about 160 labors, most of which were from outside the community, but now because of the war, operations have been cut back and production is handled by the workers that live here. I also learned that in exchange for leaving the plantations in peace, the local Viet Cong were extorting a quota of raw rubber bales from each of the five plantations in the area. This cut the profits of the plantation so much that it was barely supporting its self.

I wasn't asked anything during that first meeting and had kept my two cents to myself, but I now had a clearer understanding as to Alain Forette's motives for helping the Americans. He needed the money, but he also wanted to fight back at the Viet Cong who were strangling the life out of the plantation he loves.

With Muesell gone, I had the room to myself. There were no air conditioners except for one in a window of the office. There was a large ceiling fan that kept the air moving in the room, but it was still hot, so I opened the French doors and pulled shut the long see through curtains that substituted for a screen. Restless that first night, I crawled out from under the mosquito net and turned on the bed side lamp for a moment to look at my watch. It was midnight and I decided to go outside for a smoke. I was sitting on the same bench as earlier when I notice a light come on in the room opposite. With the light behind her I could see a woman in a negligee standing in the doorway of the room across the way. It was Karen DeKemp and with the light showing through her negligee, it was like she was wearing nothing at all. It was quite a sight. She turned the light off and came outside smoking a cigarette and pacing back and forth for a couple of minutes. She didn't notice me at first, not until she was putting her cigarette out. She didn't say anything, she just waived and went back inside her room. The next night it was the same thing. She appeared in the doorway in her negligee, but this time she came across the courtyard and said she was out of cigarettes and got one of mine. We sat on the iron bench together and talked for about twenty minutes until she said goodnight and went back to her room. I waited the next night too, but she didn't come out.

Three days had past and with Muesell and Xu Tan back, I was on my way to Saigon to pick up the equipment Alain had requested.

CHAPTER 10

A Hero?

Alain was going to Saigon to pick up supplies so I caught a ride. He dropped me off in Cholon, the Chinese market district, and I caught a taxi to the embassy. After briefing Roark on the progress of the operation and giving him the list of special equipment Alain wanted, he told me that there was someone at VE-AD looking for me. It was lunch time so Jack Roark called the compound and said we would be there after lunch. We went to Jack's favorite restaurant, ate and had a cold beer. Roark was true to his word and picked up the check, then we were on our way.

When we arrived at Colonel Augden's office, he told us to have a seat and he would be right back. I lit up a smoke and offered one to Roark. We sat there for three or four minutes then the door opened. In came Colonel Augden, Captain Sullivan and Bill Morgan. I stood up and wondered what was the hell was going on. After Morgan shut the door the Colonel took a small pile of stuff off his file cabinet and placed them on his desk, then said.

"Captain Sullivan is here as your former Detachment Commander."

"First of all, Sergeant Whitley, I want to tell you that the *Statement of Charges* for the M16 you lost has been determined to be a combat loss in the line of duty." Sullivan said.

"Yes sir, I know. The Sergeant Major at the 1st Air Cav told me." I said while I was still trying to figure out what was going on.

"Well, hold on. There's more to it than that. While doing the line of duty investigation, I tracked down Lieutenant Flores at the 6th of the 31st Infantry. Based on his written statement, I then tracked down Specialist Five Murphy at the hospital here in Saigon and got his statement which I verified with the 555th Aviation Battalion. While doing this I was informed that you had been recommended for awards which were approved but Lieutenant Flores only had your last name and didn't know your unit of assignment."

"Well, to make a long story short. Due to the work put in by Captain Sullivan you have been awarded the following medals. The Air Medal with combat V, upon recommendation of the Commander of the 555th

Aviation. For your action prior to and immediately after the crash, upon joint recommendation of the 6th of the 31st Infantry and the 555th Aviation, the Commanding General of the 9th Infantry Division has awarded you the Bronze Star for Valor. For your action with Bravo Company, 6th of the 31st Infantry the night of the crash and the following day, you have been awarded the Army Commendation Medal with combat V. Forwarded form the 1st Air Cavalry Division for your action as a door gunner in Operation Pegasus the Air Medal with oak leaf cluster." The Colonel finally paused for a moment and handed the certificates and presentation boxes to me. Then said. "Congratulations Sergeant Whitley."

"Thank you sir." I said as everyone else joined in with their congratulations and hand shakes. Finally the Colonel spoke up again and said.

"OK, Captain Sullivan, Mister Morgan, if you will excuse us now, we have some work to get out of the way."

I thanked the Captain for going to all the trouble to track down the paper work and when the door closed, Roark gave the Colonel the same briefing I had given him. The only question the Colonel had was when, and Roark replied, soon.

Roark dropped me off at the hotel and told me to come by his office about 1300 hours the next day and he would have the stuff I needed. I went upstairs, packed away the awards certificates and medals, took a hot shower and laid down to take a nap. Before I went to sleep, I thought about the medals I had carried up to the room and wondered if it was an omen. When I think of soldiers winning medals, it is usually about guys that have been killed. I came to Vietnam because I was ordered to, not because I wanted to win medals, and I certainly didn't want to get killed. Oh I have seen the ribbons on the uniforms of other guys, and seen the medals on the dress uniforms at military formals and parades, but I have never thought of me being one of those soldiers.

It was about 1800 hours when I awoke to Charlie coming into the room. He said he was going to take a shower then go down to the bar and have a few drinks and get something to eat. He wanted to know if I wanted to go with him. I said I did and we were soon on our way down to the hotel bar. We sat at a table with another civilian employee of the Embassy and a couple of reporters, or war correspondents as they like to be called. After dinner I grew uncomfortable with the direction of the conversation and all the questions that were being asked, like do you think we should be here, and how do you think the war is going. Offering no opinion, I excused myself by telling them I wanted to turn in early. It seemed that most of the reporters around the hotel were anti war and were always looking for something controversial to send back to their papers. It is not that I am for the war, I mean what soldier is. They just made me feel uncomfortable and from that night on, I didn't hang around the hotel bar much when I was in Saigon.

The next day I decided to walk to the Embassy. On the way there was an explosion about a half block in front of me. A bomb had been set off in one of the bars and it was utter chaos. The street was full of bodies and debris from the building. By the time I got up to the crowd that had gathered on the street MPs were starting to arrive as well as the QCs, Vietnamese Police. I could hear multiple sirens getting closer, so there was little I could do to help out. I skirted my way around the crowd and continued on to the Embassy which was in lock down. It took me a few minutes, but I finally got inside, everything was being searched, even more so than usual.

In Jack's office he didn't waste any time. Everything was arranged. My instructions were to take the Duc Phan Taxi to the *flower shop* and pick up an order for Son Tran, then on to the plantation. Simple enough I thought, but when I got outside the Embassy and crossed the street the Duc Phan Taxi was no where to be seen. I fended off the other taxi drivers wanting a fare and walked down to the corner where the restaurant Jack had taken me to was and sat out side and ordered a beer. There was still a lot of commotion and sirens still wailing in the distance. About fifteen minutes later I saw a black taxi pull up across from the Embassy. I couldn't tell if was the right taxi so I walked back down the street to see. When I got there I saw Duc eating a bowl of noodles in the front seat. I got in the back seat and told him to take me to the *flower shop*.

After picking up a large canvas bag at the flower shop we arrived back at the plantation. The two men at the gate weren't armed, but I noticed that there were two AK47s leaning on the stone pillar on the inside of the gate. It was a mild day and the humidity was coming up, getting ready for the afternoon rain. I could see some of the workers getting off a truck at the large building and some of the women taking in wash off the clothes lines around the group of small houses. I knocked on the door and opened it as the Mister Tu was on his way to answer it. Tu had been the personal valet of Cia's father and Cia has known him all her life. He and his wife are more like members of the family than servants.

"Hello Mister Tu, looks like it's going to rain today."

"Rain every day." He replied as he reached for the canvas bag I was carrying.

"No, that's OK, I've got it. What are the chances of a cold glass of ice tea."

Tu just smiled and bowed before leaving the room for the kitchen. I walked down the hall to my and Muesell's room, dropped the bag on the foot of the bed. I opened the French doors and went outside to smoke. I was seated on the iron bench when Tu arrived with my tea, it was way too sweet for me so I handed it back to him and said.

"Too sweet."

"*Toot sweet.*" Tu said as he turned around and started to hurry back to the kitchen. Toot sweet is Vietnamese for the French phrase *tout de suite* meaning, roughly, right now.

"No. Mister Tu, not toot sweet. Too sweet, too much sugar." I said as I stuck my finger into the glass he was holding and put it in my mouth while shaking my head no."

I still don't think he understood what I was talking about, but he took the tea and headed back to the kitchen. I guess I'll find out if he brings me a glass back. Language can be a problem sometimes, but it is only a problem for me. After all, they speak Vietnamese.

Delbert's wife was playing games with some of the children at the end of the courtyard by the big iron gate when it started to rain. I just sat there for a moment in the rain and watched the kids scurry off through the gate. I figured it wouldn't be long before the men came to the house so I decided to take a shower before dinner.

Just as I was finishing up in the bathhouse in came Alain and Muesell.

"Good, you're back. Did you bring me a present?" Alain asked.

"I did. It's in the room."

"Good, we will see to it after dinner. I think you will like the plan, it is almost too easy."

I acknowledged Alain and headed back to the room. I didn't like the sound of the plan being too easy. The only thing too easy over here is getting dead, and I wasn't ready for that one yet.

On my way back to the room, I noticed Brian and Karen DeKemp on the other side of courtyard outside their rooms. They appeared to be arguing about something, but I really couldn't hear what they were saying. Finally Karen turned her back on Brian and went to her room. Brian saw me watching them, I waved at him, but he turned his back on me and went to his room. Embarrassed, I guess.

Muesell and Karen DeKemp were both missing from dinner. I wondered what was going on, but kept my mouth shut and figured that if it concerned me, I would be told. Dinner was excellent, though it was a little subdued, conversation wise. Cia seemed to be preoccupied and was sharper than usual with the girl serving the food. She was the mistress of the house and never let anyone forget it for an instant. We were just about finished eating when Muesell came in. He nodded in Alain's direction and took his usual seat. Cia clapped her hands and instructed the girl to bring food in for Muesell.

We all lingered a little longer than usual to let Muesell eat. Finally he pushed his plate back. Cia clapped her hands and the serving girl brought out the coffee. Mister Tu was right behind her with the cognac. Alain, Muesell and Brian lit cigars and Delbert and I lit cigarettes while Borland stoked his pipe. Soon there was a cloud of smoke hovering over the table. Cia said something to Delbert's wife and they both got up from the table.

"So. No problems?" Alain directed his question to Muesell.

"No problems, except what you have to deal with here in the house." Was Muesell's cryptic response.

I wasn't the only one who didn't know what was going on. Brian DeKemp and Borland both had puzzled looks on there faces.

"Well, I have some work to complete." Delbert said as he snubbed out his cigarette and got up from the table.

After dinner while we were going over the plans for our first mission, I found out what was going on with Cia Forette. She was very unhappy about events that had taken place that day. Delbert had walked in on one of the workers going through the drawers of Alain's desk in the office. Delbert had backed back out of the office and the man hadn't noticed him. Delbert notified Alain immediately. When Alain and Muesell found and questioned the man they found the file, that I had brought from the Saigon for our first mission, stuck inside his shirt. Muesell already suspected the man of being an informant for the Viet Cong, because he was always asking a lot of questions about stuff that was none of his business. Alain had decided not to do anything except keep an eye on him because he was one of Cia's cousins. Now he had no choice but to do something.

Muesell had taken care of the problem and got rid of the man's body by dropping it off in an area that had been accidentally bombed by the ARVN Air Force last night. Alain had to tell Cia, because there is not anything that goes on at the plantation that she doesn't find out about. Alain knew she would be upset, but would be more so, if he hadn't told her.

CHAPTER 11

Extreem Prejudice

The bag I had picked up at the flower shop contained two satchel charges packed with C4 plastic explosives and three different kinds of detonators, chemical pull cord type, mechanical timers, and electrical.

Our target, a Police Chief, like most people of power or money in Vietnam lived in a guarded villa with high fences. So his home as the location was discarded almost immediately by Alain. Alain went on to explain that on Muesell and Xu Tan's surveillance trip they discovered that Fang Dien Nguyen, the Chief of Police of Viet Can Province had a regular routine. He was picked up by his driver at home every morning at exactly 0800 hours. The trip to his office at Headquarters took from twenty to thirty minutes. The difference is because the driver never takes the same route to the Provence Headquarters. This fact also ruled out any kind of ambush.

"There is one thing that the driver does almost everyday prior to picking up the Chief."

"What's that." I asked.

"After picking up the car at Provence Headquarters he almost always stops at a restaurant to eat." Alain said.

"I think his wife works there." Muesell added.

"You said. Almost always stops." "Not every day?" I asked.

Muesell interjected again. "Xu Tan says that he never orders, the girl just brings him food. It has to be his wife or girl friend the way she talks to him. Telling him not to be late and stuff."

"Anyway, he stops often enough for us to use this information." Alain said then continued. "He parks the car in the alley beside the restaurant, there are no windows so he can't see the car."

"But not every day." I said.

"It doesn't make any difference. If he doesn't stop the day we are ready, then we just try again the next day. It is easy enough to do. While the car is in the alley, with a little distraction so no one sees, we simply walk up and put a satchel charge on a timer set for 0815 in the boot of the car. It's a Fiat, there is no lock on the boot, you just push the button and open it." Alain Forette seemed pleased with his presumably fool proof plan.

Well the plan was simple, it had that going for it. The simpler a plan the fewer things that can go wrong, but fool proof, no plan is fool proof. For the life of me, I couldn't find anything wrong with it, so I agreed. Alain called the flower shop on the phone and left the message in Vietnamese, "Tell the Chef that the kitchen has his order ready." So now we just had to wait for the message from the flower shop to say, "The order is ready to be picked up." It was getting late and would be at least tomorrow before we heard anything.

Delbert knocked on the door to the office and stuck his head in. "Are you guys ready to play cards?" Apparently, this was the men's poker night. Now I love playing poker, and I was invited to do so, but I just didn't feel like it tonight. So while Alain, Muesell, Brian, Borland and Delbert walked back to the kitchen to play cards I walked with them to get another cup of coffee. I watched them play for a few minutes then walked back to my room.

Sitting on the iron bench outside the room drinking my coffee and smoking a cigarette I noticed a light on in Karen DeKemp's room across the courtyard. I was thinking about walking over to see why she had not been at dinner. Before I got up, she appeared at the door, lingered for a moment then came outside. I waved at her and she walked across and sat on the bench with me. I offered her a cigarette to break the ice.

"I noticed you weren't at dinner this evening." I said as I lit the cigarette for her.

"I didn't feel like eating. I never feel like eating after a fight with my brother."

"I know it's none of my business, and you don't have to tell me if you don't want to, but…."

"It was about you." She said, confusing the hell out of me.

"Me. I don't understand."

"Brian doesn't like you. He doesn't like any man I take an interest in or like. He just has to understand that I am not a little girl anymore. I'm a grown woman and I'll see whom ever I want to, and it's none of his business." She continued as the flood gates were now open. "I'm twenty four and he still treats me like I was twelve years old. I told him he is my brother and I love him, but that does not give him the right to interfere in my personal life."

"How did he take it?" I asked and immediately wished I had just let it drop.

"He didn't like it, but I think we have an understanding now."

"And do you?" I asked.

"Do I what?" She replied.

"Like me, or have an interest in me."

"You know I hadn't thought about it much, until he told me to stay away from you. Now I think I do." She said as she leaned over and kissed me.

I liked it and I kissed her again. A few moments later, as the sun was going down, we were walking across the courtyard to her room to celebrate her new found liberation.

Two hours of lust and Karen was now asleep. I got dressed and started back to my room. It was really dark as it was a new moon and I only had the light in my room to guide me until my eyes adjusted to the night. I noticed the light was still on in the kitchen. I could hear the sounds of the poker game still going and was glad to see that Muesell was not in the room. I was going to sleep good this night.

The next day at breakfast everyone seemed to be in good spirits, especially Karen who was in a real cheerful mood. Delbert was the big winner at the poker game and was enjoying rubbing it in the faces of the other guys who were taking it well enough. Cia was still upset about her cousin, but seem to be accepting the fact that it had to be done. It was about 1400 hours when the call came from the flower shop. It was a go.

We could leave about 0500 hours in the morning and arrive in plenty of time to do the deed, but we would have problems and too many questions at the road blocks. So we decided to drive up to Viet Can and spend the night. Alain asked Cia to make the arrangements with a relative of hers, the local Doctor, for us to spend the night. We drove both of the cars at the plantation.

Muesell, Brian and Borland in the Fiat. Alain and I in the old Renault. Our gear was packed under the back seats in both cars with nothing in the trunks, that were commonly searched at the road blocks. If we had any problems at the checkpoints my VE-AD ID card should get us through. Muesell and I were wearing side arms and those were the only weapons showing.

We arrived at Doctor Din Van Lat's villa in the town of Tan Thoi Nhut, Viet Can Provence about 1730 hours that afternoon. The Doctor seemed nervous and his wife wasn't happy at all about our being there. We parked both of the cars inside the gates and were shown to an old carriage house. The Doctor moved his car out, and a girl brought out several rolled up reed mats for us to sleep on then returned with some tea. Alain had not recognized the girl at first until she spoke to him. It was then he realized that the girl was the Doctor's oldest daughter that he hadn't seen in four years. Alain ate dinner in the house that night, the rest of us stayed in the carriage house with our equipment and food was brought out to us.

The next morning we were all a little on edge as we pulled out and headed for the restaurant. We didn't want to get there too early someone might notice us just sitting around, but we had to be there early enough to catch the driver. We took the Fiat with Alain driving and Brian in the front seat. Muesell and I were in the back seat. We all had pistols and there were two loaded AK47s in the car, just in case we had to make a forced getaway. Sig Borland had stayed at the villa with the Renault and the rest of our gear. As we approached the restaurant Muesell had the satchel charge sitting on his lap with the timer set for 8:15 ready to activate. We were there in plenty of time. Alain went around the block and pulled into the alley directly across from where the driver parks.

We waited. Something was wrong. It was getting too late for the driver and we were getting ready to leave when he showed up. The driver didn't park, he just pulled up in front of the restaurant and blew his horn. A woman brought out something wrapped in newspaper and handed it to the driver and he pulled away. Aborted for the day we returned to the villa. Hopefully we will be out of here tomorrow. Doctor Lat's wife was really giving him hell about us spending another night. We could hear her yelling at him from inside the carriage house.

None of us got much sleep that night except Borland who could sleep through anything. Muesell spent half the night cleaning weapons and double and triple checking all the gear. The next morning we tried again. This time the driver was on time and parked beside the restaurant in the alley. As soon as the driver went inside Alain pulled across the street and stopped right behind the other Fiat. Muesell activated the timer, got out of the car and placed the satchel charge in the trunk up against the back seat on the passenger side and got back in the car. The whole thing took less than a minute. Muesell then directed Alain to a location over looking the front of Fang Dien Nguyen's villa.

The driver showed up at exactly 0800 hours and the gates were opened for him. Three minutes later the driver pulls out with Chief Nguyen in the back seat. Alain tried to follow the car at a distance, but lost sight of the car.

He then headed in the general direction of the Provence Headquarters building. Alain found a place just down the road and pulled over to wait. At 0812 hours, to our utter astonishment, Chief Nguyen's car was right beside us held up in traffic. In what seemed like an eternity, but in fact was only about 30 seconds, the car started to slowly move in the direction of the Headquarters building. Brian said the driver was too early and they would arrive at the Chief's office before the charge went off. Before we could contemplate what Brian had just said, there was a horrendous explosion just out of sight in front of us. They had not reached the Headquarters.

Alain started the car and turned onto the side street just in front of us so we could make our getaway before the streets were totally blocked. We returned to the Doctor's villa, repacked our gear under the backseats of the two cars and headed back to the plantation. Before leaving, Alain had given Doctor Lat some money. The Doctor and his wife hadn't known what we were up to, but it wouldn't take long for them to put two and two together. We didn't have to worry about them saying anything, apart from the fact that Alain's wife is a relative of the Lat's, there was nothing they could say without implicating themselves.

We were stopped at a checkpoint before getting out of Viet Can Provence. We were made to get out of the cars and open the trunks. Fortunately it was a joint ARVN and US checkpoint so I showed my ID to the Army MP and explained that Alain and Muesell were part of a French aid program that was going to setup a health clinic in conjunction with a Lutheran mission.

Brian DeKemp and Borland were with the Lutheran church. He believed my story, even though we didn't have any paperwork. The MP stopped the ARVNs from continuing the search and let us go.

We returned to the plantation to find out that Delbert had received a visit from the local Viet Cong commander the pervious night. They were looking for Cia's cousin, their inside man. Delbert said they were pissed when they couldn't find him and raided the food larders of the workers. When the VC left they took a sixteen year old boy with them, as well as the rice and two young pigs they stole. The whole plantation was in an uproar about the boy being taken. The boy wouldn't be killed, he would be held for ransom. If for some reason we couldn't buy him back the VC would just keep him as a conscript. Out of respect for Cia, the only person to enter the plantation house itself, was the commander. The main house was not searched and we were fortunate that none of the workers knew what happened to Cia's cousin.

Alain has to go back to Saigon tomorrow to replace the rice and pick up supplies, so I will catch a ride with him.

CHAPTER 12

Collateral Damage

Just like the last trip, Alain dropped me off in Cholon, and I caught a taxi and headed to the Embassy.

In Roark's office I returned the file on the Police Chief, and brought Jack up to date on how the mission went and the occurrences at the plantation.

"How much to you think the man found out about what was going on?" Jack asked.

"Well, it doesn't make any difference. According to Muesell and Delbert Foo he never had a chance to get any information out."

"And the body hasn't been found."

"If it has, it hasn't been identified or connected with the plantation." I said relying on what I was told.

"What about that story you told at the checkpoint. I like it. It was quick thinking on your part, but could have backfired. Before you go back, stop at VE-AD operations and see what they can do about identification papers for the team."

"Yes sir." I replied then continued. "What about their pay and expenses?"

"What kind of expenses are we talking about?"

"The Doctor in Tan Thoi Nhut had to be paid off and the cost of gas for the cars." I didn't know whether Jack would come across or not, but I thought I'd ask. After all, it wasn't his money.

"OK, I'll throw in an extra $500. Tell Forette that $7500 will be deposited tomorrow in his account at the Hong Kong Bank of Saigon. How he distributes the money is his business. No bonus on this one though, too much collateral damage."

"Collateral damage?" I asked.

"You didn't know? Besides the target and driver, you killed seven civilians and injured about ten more."

"No. I didn't know."

"Well sometime things can't be helped, but try and keep it under control. They don't get paid by the body count." Jack went to his safe and took out a file in a sealed envelope and a regular sized envelope and tossed them to me. "Your next target is in Rach Gau, the Deputy Governor, and here is some expense money for you. Come on, I'll give you a ride over to VE-AD. I need to see Augden anyway.

At operations I talked to Big M and explained what I needed as far as IDs for the team. Morgan gave me a Polaroid camera and told me to take head shots and write physical descriptions and names on the back of the photos. "And Whitley, don't forget to bring my camera back." He reminded me as I was leaving the office.

I checked in with Colonel Augden while I was there. He didn't have much to say, just acknowledged my sticking my head in the door. Roark was still there so I closed the door. On the taxi ride to the hotel, I looked inside the small envelope Jack had given me. It contained about eighty bucks in Vietnamese money. "What a cheap ass." I thought to myself.

I had dinner at the hotel then ran into Charlie when I stopped by the bar for a drink. There was a buzz going around between the reporters and some of the Embassy staff about the bombings. Someone mentioned the one in Viet Can, and the general feeling was the VC have turned to the bombings since they lost so many men during the January attacks. "What better place to kill foreigners than right here at the hotel." Another reporter said as kind of a joke, but then things got real quiet as people thought about it. I wanted to turn-in early so I left Charlie in the bar and headed upstairs.

I got up early the next day and walked back to the Embassy to find Duc Phan and his taxi. After arriving at the plantation, I walked in on a rather headed discussion about what to do about the boy who had been taken by the VC. I couldn't believe they were actually considering not paying the ransom to get the boy back. Brian DeKemp and Sig Borland were in favor of paying the ransom. Cia and Delbert were against it and Alain was somewhere in the middle. So as usual I butted in with my two cents worth.

"How much do they want for him?" I asked.

"Stay out of this. It does not concern you." Muesell spoke up.

"No, no, it is OK." Alain said.

"They want 7,000P or they keep the boy." Borland said.

"That's only seventy dollars. Why not pay them. I don't know the boy, but he's got to be worth more than seventy dollars." That must have been the wrong thing to say. They all started talking at once.

"I told you to stay out of this. You don't know what you are talking about." Muesell spoke up again.

"Look. It is not the money. If we pay them too soon or too easily. They will keep coming back and take more of the workers." Alain explained.

"That's why we can't pay. We will probably loose him to the Army in six months anyway." Delbert said.

"Muesell is right, this is none of my business. I have our next assignment when you are ready. I'll be in my room." I said to Alain and left the kitchen to go lay down for a while.

I couldn't sleep, I just laid there and listened to the rumble of the argument still going on in the kitchen. Finally it got quiet and I heard footsteps coming down the hall. It was Alain Forette.

"Come on. Let's see what you have for us."

I followed Alain to the office, handed him the large envelope and sat down across from his desk. I watched as he opened the envelope and studied the paper work within. Slowly he looked at each page and put it aside. He laid the photographs out and placed them side by side.

"This is a rather detailed surveillance report. It looks like they have suspected him for a long time." Alain said as he finally broke the silence.

"The powers that be said they liked the bombing because it got blamed on the VC, but complained because so many others got killed." I said while I watched for a change in Alain's expression, to see how he took the information.

Alain looked up from the papers and said something in French then translated it for me as. "To get to market, sometimes you have to whip the donkey." It didn't make much since to me and I took it to mean something like the American expression, *you can't make an omelet without breaking some eggs.*

We were joined by the rest of the men, with the exception of Delbert. Alain pushed the papers across the desk for them to look over. Finally the silence was broken by Sig Borland.

"I don't think we can do this from here, it is too far." Borland said.

"I agree with Sig, it is just too far for us to operate from here, just too much time on the road after, too dangerous. We almost got caught at a check point last time." Muesell said.

"About that. *Chef* said he liked the idea of identification that would make it reasonable for us to be in the area. So I brought back a camera that will take head shots and they will make ID cards for us." I interjected.

"That's good, but it is still too far for us to operate. There is an American base not far from the town of Dut Hoa. See if *Chef* can make arrangements for us to stay there for a while." Alain said then continued. OK then, that about covers it for now, except for the photos Whitley wants to take."

I took the head shots with the camera and annotated the information Big M wanted on the back of them. I was careful to change the background each time so the ID cards wouldn't look like they were all made at the same time.

Coming back from the shower room I passed Karen on her way to the kitchen. She whispered in a low voice as we passed. "Tonight my room, midnight."

I found out at dinner that night that Alain had decided not to ransom the boy and just let him become a new recruit for the VC. I thought it was a wrong decision, but it really was none of my business so I kept my mouth shut this time. Dinner was good and the conversation contained itself to the plantation operations with Delbert doing most of the talking. That's when we found out that Delbert's wife was pregnant again. I'll say this, the climate in this country does nothing to dissuade the men and women from their lust.

That night Muesell was snoring away and dead to the world so I went outside to have a smoke and wait for midnight. At about 5 minutes till, a small light came on in Karen's room. All was quiet, the only other people awake on the plantation were the two guards at the front gate and the two at the back gate. I felt like a thief in the night as I made my way across the courtyard. In other circumstances Karen may have only been average in appearance, but for me tonight she is the most beautiful woman in the world. After two and a half hours of lust in the night, I returned to my room, with Muesell still snoring, thoroughly satisfied, exhausted and soaking wet with sweat. I grabbed my towel off the hook on the wall and went back to the shower room.

The next day I got Muesell to give me a ride to Saigon. As usual I got out in Cholon and caught a cyclo taxi to the Embassy. Roark's office was locked and I walked back down the hall to where Charlie works. He said Jack was around so I went down to the basement to get a cup of coffee. While there Jack walked in, saw me, got some coffee and joined me. I gave him the list that Alain had given me before I left the plantation.

"The sniper rifle is no problem, but I'll have to get the two pistols with silencers from my contacts with the

Navy Seals. May take a while." Jack said as he put the list in the breast pocket of his jacket and I wondered how many of those cheap looking seersucker suits he has. He reminded me of a Louisiana politician and just about as crooked.

Not having anything else to discuss with Jack, I left the Embassy and caught a taxi to the VE-AD compound. I stopped in the operations room and gave the photos and camera back to Big M. He told me it would take about an hour to get the ID cards made. Down the hall I knocked on Colonel Augden's door.

"Come in Whitley, have a seat."

"Thank you, Sir." I said and took the seat next to his desk instead of the one across the room.

"Well tell me Sergeant how are things going with you?" Augden asked and seemed to be in an unusually good mood as he took a Kool from the pack on his desk and lit it.

I started to brief him on the last operation but he stopped me.

"No. I mean you. How are you doing? Are you holding up okay, is everything going alright, do you need anything you're not getting? To point, is there anything that I can do for you?" Augden asked, and almost made me believe he really cares.

"Everything is fine with me, but there is something I need."

"Look, Sergeant Whitley, I understand you went on the mission. That was not part of the original plan. You are suppose to be the middleman. As it turned out, it was a good thing you were along. But, you understand that if you get caught, you are on your own and we never heard of you. Now, what is it that you need."

"It's the job in Rash Gau. We need a base of operations closer to the situation. There is a army base in Dut Hoa, and I wonder if you can arrange for the team to stay there for a week or so."

"The base is actually in Rash Kien, part of the 9th Infantry. Dut Hoa is only an artillery fire support base. In any case I'll make the arrangements and let Jack know. Is there anything else?"

"No sir, that about covers it." I said as stood up to leave. Just as I was about to walk out the door, Augden had one more thing to say.

"Whitley. Do what you have to do, you are the man in the field, but cover your ass."

That's right. CYA, *cover your ass* seems to be the main priority of everyone over here above the rank of private. I already knew that my ass would be in the wind if I got caught, but somewhere in the back of my mind I knew they would never abandon me, or, maybe that's just me being naive.

While picking up the identification cards from operations, Big M told me Roark called and said to stop by the flower shop before I went back tomorrow. I had been thinking about going back tonight, but that would be pushing the curfcw so I walked down to the hotel.

I ate a burger and fries at the bar for dinner, along with a couple of drinks. As I was ordering my third a woman took the stool next to me and said.

"I have seen you here before." As she held a cigarette and waited for me to light it. I did, and she followed with. "My name is Ling. Would you like to buy me a drink?"

"Sure, why not." I said and motioned to the bartender. "And how is Ling doing this evening?"

"I could be doing better. I am lonely. Are you lonely?" She asked.

Now this is not one of your local B girls that work the clubs. The girls that work the hotels are dressed to kill and stone beautiful. Ling was no exception. She had her hair piled high on her head and was wearing high heels and dressed in a soft green silk dress with a slit running to mid thigh on her left leg, and like I said, she was beautiful. Normally I would have jumped at a chance to be with a girl that looked this good, but my head was somewhere else at the time. So I shined her on for a while then paid for the drinks and went upstairs, by myself.

Charlie was on his way out to play cards when I got to the room, he asked me if I wanted to join him. I declined, telling him I had an early start in the morning.

The next day, I showered and shaved then headed down stairs to the restaurant for breakfast. I was starved and ordered almost every thing on the menu. I walked back toward the Embassy to find Duc Phan and his taxi. The taxi was just pulling in when I arrived, but there was a different driver.

"Sorry, I was looking for Duc Phan." I said to the driver.

"It OK, I Duc Phan." The man responded.

"Where is the other driver?" I asked.

"It OK, I tell you. I Duc Phan, have two more taxi. My brother drive one and my wife her brother drive one. It OK, I tell you. I Duc Phan."

"Do you work for the Embassy?"

"Yes. All same, same. All Duc Phan taxi special taxi. It OK, I tell you."

"I want to go to Phu Thanh, but I need to stop by the flower shop first. Do you know the flower shop?"

"Yes, yes, I know. I tell you we special taxi."

"You big CIA man. Right."

Well, that caught me off guard. I had to think, before I responded, then said. "No, I work for VE-AD, I help farmers. You know farmers?"

"You don't look like you work in rice paddy."

"I don't plant rice. I help the farmers who plant the rice."

"OK, you boss." He said, but I don't think he believed me.

I can't wait until I tell Jack about this. We stopped and I made my pick-up at the flower shop. When I came out Duc was listing to AFVN on the radio. I hoped that would keep him from talking so much. Then on across the river to Phu Thanh and the Foo Hanh Rubber Plantation.

It was almost noon when I arrived and everyone was sitting down to lunch. I held up the long package I was carrying to show Alain and continued on down the hall to my room.

CHAPTER 13

Mystry Woman

Alain was pleased with the sniper rifle I brought back from Saigon, it was an Austrian made bolt action 303 equipped with a scope, and sound and flash suppresser. Both Alain and Muesell had used similar weapons in the Legion. In the office, I handed out the IDs and papers provided by Big M. All four of the men were identified as employees of the International Red Cross. I relayed the information about Chef wanting to hold down the collateral damage. Alain said that the method of carrying out the mission would be determined by the circumstances and nothing else.

The following day we received word that arrangements for our stay at the army base had been made and we were off to the Delta and Rash Kien. Rash Kien wasn't as close as Dut Hoa, but it was close enough for our purposes. We settled into the hooch that had been provided and ate our meals in the Infantry Battalion mess hall. The guards became familiar with us driving on and off the base everyday to do our own surveillance in Rash Gau. All the back ground information and surveillance work that was included in the mission package was damn accurate, and our own surveillance added little to it.

After the fourth day, Alain decided we had no choice but to the take the target out with a shot in daylight from the car. Muesell was the obvious choice to make the shot since he had been a sniper in the Legion. We used both cars just in case we needed a back-up for a getaway. The target made a stop in the crowded market in Dut Hoa every night on his way home and would get out of his car and walk around on foot. The market was dangerous, but it was the only thing he did consistently. We hoped in the confusion we would be able to get away with out being seen.

With Borland and DeKemp in the back-up car and with Alain driving the Fiat with me in the front as a spotter and Muesell in the backseat with the rifle we drove through the market on the main road. The other drivers on the road would occasionally just stop and make purchases from the vegetable and fish stands, so we would pull over frequently while we were waiting for the target's car.

Finally I spotted the target's car stopped at one of the stands. The target was still in the car in the back seat and the driver was out buying something at one of stands. We didn't need the rifle, the driver's window was down and Alain pulled up slowly beside the car and only stopped momentarily as Muesell lightly tossed a grenade into the open driver's window. I don't think the target even noticed. About eight seconds later as we were now about three car lengths ahead of the car the grenade exploded and the Deputy Governor of Rash Gau province was dead. We passed the back-up car and Borland pulled out behind us and stopped the car to slow any traffic behind us. While we were still moving Muesell stowed the rifle and the other grenade he had out, back under the back seat. I was still armed with my pistol, but I passed Alain's semi-automatic to Muesell for him to hide. We drove normally back to the base at Rash Kien and we were worried about Borland and DeKemp because they should have caught up to us on the road.

Borland and DeKemp arrived at the army base about 30 minutes after us. They had stopped and joined the crowd at the market trying to see what had happened. Borland confirmed that the target was dead, along with three other people with four more wounded by the explosion. No one seemed to know what happened, except that the car exploded.

I knew Roark wouldn't be happy with the additional causalities, but the mission was accomplished. The next morning, Alain broke down the 303 for me and we stowed it in a duffle bag along with the mission file and the other two grenades and a satchel charge that we had brought with us, as well as extra ammunition and incidentals that the four Red Cross workers shouldn't have with them. I took the duffle bag and with my priority travel orders caught a helicopter back to Saigon. The other guys drove the cars back to the plantation.

Back at the hotel, I stowed the duffle bag in the closet of my room. I went down stairs to get something to eat and called Jack Roark's office to see how long he was going to be in.

It was late afternoon when I arrived at the Embassy and returned the file on the Deputy Governor. When I told Jack about Duc Phan and the conversation I had with him in the taxi, he laughed.

"You didn't admit to anything did you?" He asked while still laughing.

"No. Of course not."

"Don't worry about it. He does that to every one. Duc Phan thinks he is the second coming of James Bond. With the money I pay him each month, he wouldn't dare cross me. Besides, the Vietnamese think that every US civilian over here works for the CIA, including me." He laughed again.

I started to fill Jack in on how the operation went, but he stopped me.

"I know. I've already been briefed. Too bad about the civilians, but we knew this one was going to be a difficult one going in." Jack said as he got up and went to his safe and retrieved two large envelopes.

"These two should be easier. The order in which they are done is your choice." Jack said as he handed me the files and went back to his desk and got two more letter size envelopes. "Expenses." He said as he tossed me the envelopes and continued. "Tell Forette his money is already in the bank, and before you go back tomorrow check at the flower shop there is another package for you. Now, unless you have something else for me. I have a date." With that, Jack got his suite jacket off the coat rack, and I made my departure.

Back at the hotel for the night, I stuck the envelopes in the duffle bag, with the exception of the one that had Viking hand written on it. My expense money, another eighty bucks. Wow, I said to myself. Charlie wasn't in the room, but I could tell he had been there. I took a shower then headed down to the bar to have a drink or two before turning in.

When I arrived at the bar I noticed Ling, the good looking girl I had met when I was in before, sitting at a table with Charlie. I really didn't think much about it. I mean, after all, she is a working girl. I order a whisky and coke then felt something touch my left shoulder. I turned to see who it was and was surprised to see Ling using the back of my of the stool I was sitting on to help her climb onto the barstool next to me. She must have gotten up from the table with Charlie as soon as she saw me come in.

"Hello again." She said as she situated her dress and got out one of her American cigarettes.

"Hi." I replied. "Can I buy you a drink?" I asked as I admired the dress she was wearing. It was a modern silk oriental style evening dress with the long slit up the side and sleeveless. I was so distracted, it took me a moment to realize she was waiting for mc to light her cigarette.

"Thank you but, let me buy your drink. If you don't mind." She said and smiled seductively.

Now I'm young, but have traveled enough to be familiar with working girls, and this is the first time I have ever had one buy me a drink. She must be expensive. I thought to myself, if she can afford to buy the customer drinks. As good looking as this gal is, she would never have to buy a drink in a bar, even if she wasn't a working girl. She paid for the drinks when the bartender sat them down then excused herself to go to the powder room. While she was away, I wondered if I had her pegged all wrong. When Ling returned, she moved her stool closer to mine, before she climbed onto it. The conversation consisted of general chitchat, with questions like how do I like Vietnam, was I married and where am I from in the States. It wasn't until the second round of drinks, that she also paid for, the questions started getting around to where I worked and what did I do. I thought about asking her what she did for a living, to see what she would say. I didn't have to, she told me that works for the Vietnamese government at the Board of Trade as a translator, and besides speaking English, she also speaks Chinese, French, and a little Japanese. Boy did I feel stupid. I thought she was just another hotel girl on the make.

"Do you like seafood? There is a really good restaurant next to where I live." She asked and I hesitated. "It is close. We can walk and I hate to eat alone."

"Only if you let me buy dinner." I said and she smiled that seductive smile of hers.

We walked about a block and a half to the restaurant and I was starting to feel the drinks. She was right the food was excellent, and we had rice wine with the lobster and mixed drinks after the meal. No matter what the conversation was, it always ended with Ling asking questions about my job. The restaurant had a lot of customers when we came in, but I realized we were the only customers left when the manager came over and said something in Vietnamese to Ling.

"I am sorry, I was enjoying myself so much, I forgot about the time. We have missed curfew, but you can say with me."

"I don't want to put you to any trouble."

"Please. It is no trouble, it is my mistake for not keeping track of the time." She said and I noticed the manager still waiting. I figured he wanted to be paid so I took out my wallet. "No no, it is my fault. I will pay, please."

"I wouldn't think of it." I said as I continued to open my wallet. I showed her some money and she took one of the twenties and gave it to the manager.

"We better go through the kitchen so we don't get the manager in trouble. It connects to my building." She said and I followed her through the kitchen and into hallway leading to the lobby of the hotel next door. It was a hotel, but it also had resident apartments. Hers was on the second floor and I could really feel the booze as we climbed the stairs. The apartment was small, but really nice. It consisted of a bedroom and living room with one of those tiny all-in-one kitchen units, and a western style bathroom and shower. After the brief tour she led me to the sofa and asked me if I wanted another drink.

"No, I think I've had enough booze for one night." I said then went for it. I figured no guts no glory.

I took her by the hands and pulled her down to my lap and kissed her. She coyly protested briefly then joined in. After about ten minutes petting on the sofa she stood up and said that she had to work early in the morning. Well, I figured that was it for the night, but she took *me* by the hands this time and led me into the bedroom and sat me on the bed. She went into the bathroom and left the door partially opened. She disappeared behind the door for about a minute. The next time I saw her she had a towel wrapped around her and was at the sink taking off her make-up, contacts and false eyelashes. She let her hair down and brushed it a few times then came and stood in front of me between my legs and started to unbutton my shirt. From that point there were no mixed signals in my mind. I undressed and she led me to the bathroom. With her hair down and out of her high heels, she was a tiny thing, but still beautiful, even without her make-up. We showered together with her washing me all over. With Vietnamese women it is all about pleasing their man, so I have been told. After the shower and in the bed, she certainly did.

The next morning I didn't open my eyes, but I could hear Ling in the shower. When I did open my eyes she was dressed and ready to go to work.

Ronald E. Whitley

"Be sure and lock the door when you leave. Will I see you tonight?"

"I can't. I will be gone for a few days.

"Where are you going? You can tell me that can't you?"

"Sure, but I don't know yet. I'll find out this morning."

"You will tell me when you get back, otherwise I might think you do not want to see me again." She said acting like I hurt her feelings.

"Of course I want to see you again and I'll tell you what ever you want to know when I get back."

"Be sure and lock the door. I am going to be late." With that she blew me a kiss and hurried out of the apartment.

I got up and washed my face and gargled with some mouth wash she had in the bathroom. When I got dressed I noticed something odd. My wallet was on the wrong side, I always carry it in my right hip pocket and never on the left, because I am right handed. I opened it and checked my money. It was all there as near as I could tell. If she did take any money, it couldn't have been more than a dollar or two. The only other thing I had in there was my Department of Defense civilian ID card. My VE-AD ID was in my hotel room. It could be my imagination, but I had the feeling she had looked in it. Or, it could just be an excuse for me, being the nosy bastard that I am, to poke through her things.

It was strange, she had a closet full of clothes and about a dozen pair of shoes. One of the drawers in the dresser in the bedroom was full of nightgowns, bras and underwear, the rest of the drawers were empty. The top of the dresser had some hair clips and combs, and a few perfume bottles. In the bathroom there was a clothes hamper with the clothes she wore last night draped over it, some personal toiletries and make-up with a robe hanging on the back of the door. The rest of the apartment was the same way. There was none of the other stuff. No books or magazines, no pictures or personal papers, no junk or knickknacks that people collect. In fact it reminded me of my hotel room. Except for my clothes there was nothing in the room to show anyone lives there except Charlie.

I left her place and headed back down the street to the hotel. In the room I was surprised to find Charlie still there.

"Hey Charlie, not working today." I said as I went to the closet to get ready to return to the plantation.

"I've got duty officer tonight. I go in at 6 and get off tomorrow morning. What I want to know is what did you do. I mean every guy in the place has hit on her. Oh, she might talk to them for a while, but no go. So what I want to know is what makes you so special? She has never left the bar with anyone before, that I know of. So what gives?"

"I don't know. You seemed to be pretty close to her when I came in."

"Yeah, talking about you!"

"What do you mean, talking about me?"

"Nothing really. It's like she really likes you and asked a lot of questions."

"What kind of questions?" I asked and he could tell I was getting irritated.

"You know man. Girl questions, like who are you, where do you work, what do you do. It's like she is trying to find out if you are one of the big dogs."

"What did you tell her?"

"Nothing really important."

"What does that mean?"

"I told her that I share a room with you, that you work for the Economic Development Agency and you are gone a lot. That's all. Did I do something wrong?"

"Yeah. You blew my cover." I said then laughed to put him at ease. "If she knows that I share a room with you, then she knows that I couldn't possibly be one of the big dogs."

I finished getting the stuff ready to take back to the plantation. On the way out Charlie said.

"Hey, you never did tell me. How did it go last night?"

I didn't answer him. I just looked at him, winked and smiled then left the room. I walked down to the Embassy and was glad to see the regular driver, he didn't talk as much as the guy I had last time. I was in no mood for conversation on this trip. We stopped at the flower shop and I picked up a package, then we headed to the plantation. On the way I was deep in thought about last night. It didn't make any since to me. A beautiful woman is asking questions about me, picks me up at the bar, buys the drinks, offers to buy dinner, and takes me to bed. So what's so unusual about that, I said to myself. Yeah right. What's not unusual about that. I knew there was something that I was not getting, but I couldn't put my finger on it.

Delbert was the only one of the guys in the house when I got there and he was busy in the office. Since I was still tired from the night before, I went to my room to take a nap.

CHAPTER 14

Missions Continue

After dinner with the usual conversation about plantation operations and wine, lots of wine. I didn't care for the wine at first, but it grows on you and I knew enough to stop after two glasses, even though they all drink it like water. The men retired to the office and I stopped by my room to pick up the package and the envelopes I had brought in. When I arrived Muesell was pouring glasses of cognac.

"What are we celebrating?" I asked as I sat the stuff I was carrying down on the desk.

"Another successful mission." Borland said as he handed me a glass of cognac.

"And another day closer to home." DeKemp added.

"Marche ou crève" Muesell said as he held up his glass.

"Yes, marche ou crève, gentlemen, march or die. We continue to the end or we parish." Alain had the last word and everyone answered the toast by drinking their cognac.

Alain opened the small envelope with the expense money, then put it in his top desk drawer. He then opened the package that contained two pistols and two silencers and sat them on the desk.

"What is this crap, they don't fit." Borland said as he picked up one of each and tried to put them together.

Muesell mumbled something in French then took the silencer Borland was holding and screwed it on to the other pistol. "Two different kinds. One screws on and the other you push on and twist."

"Oh." Is all Borland said as I'm sure he was feeling like a moron. Of course, I wouldn't have known the difference either.

Next, Alain opened both of the larger envelopes. Paused a minute while he looked them over, then looked up.

"So, are we doing two at a time now?"

"Chef said the order is your choice." I told him.

"Have you read these?" Alain asked as he looked up at me.

"Well this one is a woman and this one is an army officer." Alain said as he laid the files out on the desk for the others to see.

"A woman?" Brian DeKemp spoke up as he reached for the cognac bottle.

"Makes no difference, as long as the money is the same." Muesell said.

"Maybe we can do them together. The woman owns a club in Cholon and the ARVN Major is her lover. I think maybe you know him. He is assigned to the Vietnamese Economic Agriculture Development Agency. That is where you work Whitley." "So do you know him?" Alain said as he handed me the photograph.

I looked at the photograph, but the man didn't look familiar to me. I just shook my head no and handed it back to him.

"Well, let me study these documents for a while and see what I can come up with." Alain said and pushed his glass toward Muesell for him to pour more cognac.

"Alain. Can I see you in private for a moment?" Delbert said as he knocked and opened the door to the office.

"Sure, we are finished in here for the time being." Alain said and motioned for us to leave.

Muesell poured himself another cognac and left the bottle on Alain's desk and we all left the room so Alain and Delbert could talk.

The afternoon rain had just finished. Muesell, Borland and Brian went back to the kitchen. Other than meals, I didn't socialize with them so I went back to my room to lay down.

It was hot and muggy when I awoke about midnight and I didn't know which was worse, the humidity or Muesell snoring away. I guess he had drank himself to sleep again, as usual. I decided to walk down to the shower to cool off. I noticed Karen's light was on in her room. I thought about walking over and tapping on her door, but she hadn't as much as make eye contact during dinner. I had only been in the shower about a minute and I heard someone come in. I was surprised because the only people who use this shower are Mister Tu and his wife and Muesell. Everyone else's bedrooms are on the other side and they use that shower. The overhead light went out and the room was only lit by the small light over the sink. I quickly washed the soap from my eyes. My heart was about to jump completely out of my chest when the stall door opened. It was Karen DeKemp.

"You scared the holy crap out of me when you turned the light out."

"Oh, scared of the dark or did you think it was Brian?" She giggled and took the towel she had wrapped around her, the only thing she was wearing, off and hung it over the stall door. She walked over took the soap out of my hand and joined me under the shower. "You don't have to worry about Brian, he and Sig are drunk and passed out in their room."

Karen was definitely feeling her oats, but she was careful to save the best for her room. It was almost four in the morning before I went back to listening to Muesell snore. I didn't have to listen to him long though. I was dead to the world almost as soon as my head hit the pillow.

I skipped breakfast the next morning and it was after lunch when Alain called us back to the office to tell us the news. The boy that had been taken by the VC was back at the plantation with no other explanation, than they let him go. Delbert figured since the VC lost their spy at the plantation, they replaced him with the boy. Alain agreed with Del's assessment, and told Delbert and Muesell to keep a close watch on him for the next few days while Alain took Sig Borland and Brian DeKemp with him to spend a few days in Saigon checking out our new targets.

Alain asked if it would be a problem for me to stay at the plantation instead of going back to Saigon because Muesell and Delbert would be out of the house during the day overseeing the rubber harvest. I told him it would be no problem because I didn't have to go back until the next mission was over, unless he needed something special from the Chef.

So I spent the next three delightful days playing footsy with Karen under the table at meals and slipping off with her every chance we thought no one would notice. Of course our midnight rendezvous continued and I thought the girl was going to wear me out. Finally the day the guys were suppose to come back, Cia informed us that she knew what was going on and we should be more discreet, because she knows how Brian feels and doesn't want any trouble in the house. Karen told her that we would be more careful in the future, and Cia smiled and went on about her business. I really don't think there is anything that goes on at the plantation that she doesn't know about.

Alain returned but he was by himself. He had just come back to pick up the pistols with the silencers. Alain said the best plan was the simplest plan. Every time the Major comes by the club, they have a couple of drinks, then go out to eat then right to her place.

"So, what is the plan?" I asked.

"The plan is, we just kill them. We hang out until the Major shows up, then we leave and go to her place to wait for them. Sig Borland had already been in her apartment twice, it's no problem. The first time he went in through a window and found a spare key. The next day we had a copy made and returned her key. So when the Major shows up at the club, we go to her place. Sig and Brian go in to wait and I stay in the car down the street. When the deed is done, they walk out the door and I pick them up. We go back to the hotel, spend the night and come back here the next day. Simple as eating bread."

"Simple as eating bread. It almost sounds too simple." I said, but I could tell Alain has his mind made up.

Simple as eating bread, what a hell of a way to describe lying in wait for two people to show up then shooting them in cold blood. Yes, I know it is war and I know it is the same thing snipers do, only not up close and personal like this. I also know that I shot that man in the warehouse in France not so long ago, but that was in self defense. And yes, I know we have blown people up with bombs and grenades, but some how this seems different and I glad I'm not the one doing it. I don't know, it just leaves a bad taste in my mouth, nothing like eating bread.

Two days later the guys returned, mission accomplished, and I headed back to Saigon to turn-in the files I had.

Jack was pleased that both jobs were done and the way they were carried out. I guess it didn't leave a bad taste in *his* mouth.

"As you know, the Major worked in operations at VE-AD. We know for sure he was releasing information. What wasn't in the report is that he may have released stuff on the K teams and about you specifically."

"What makes you think so?" I asked with some skepticism. I had begun to question everything Jack told me. I knew he would always look out for Jack, but I wasn't too sure about him always having my best interest at heart. Jack wouldn't hesitate to tell me a lie, if he thought it would help manipulate me.

"The ID cards." Jack said.

"What?"

"The Red Cross ID cards for your team. He was observed trying to make a copy of our file with the original photos attached. The copy machine in operations is about shot and was out of toner, so he slipped the file back into Big M's cabinet. Lucky for us they have such a crappy copy machine."

"What do you think he did get out with?"

"His quarters were searched this morning. We didn't find much, but these might interest you." Jack said as he handed me some photographs.

The first one was a photo of me coming out of the VE-AD supply room. The second one was also at VE-AD with me coming out of Colonel Augden's office. The third was a photo of Jack and me at the restaurant he took me to. There was some Vietnamese writing on the back of the one with me and Jack and the work Kitchen written in English.

"Besides the club owner being his girlfriend she was also his handler. Two safes were found. One at the club and one at her apartment. We don't know what is in them yet. We are having some difficulties with the Vietnamese Police, but we have the Provost Marshal working a black market angle. We can't push too hard, after all we don't want the Police to think we were involved in their demise."

"Yeah, absolutely. We don't want it coming back on us." I paused then continued. "How much do you think they know about me?"

"We're not sure. Your photos weren't the only ones. Could be just routine surveillance of the Embassy and compounds in the Saigon area." Jack said, unconvincingly.

"Excuse me Mr. Roark. These photos were taken inside the VE-AD compound and are not routine surveillance."

"Yes, I know. We still have a problem at VE-AD. We're working on it. Anyway, just in case, assuming the operational codes are compromised. *Chef* is out, you refer to me as the *Duke*. Your team is now, what else, *Viking*. Make sure Forette knows, and don't use the flower shop anymore. From now on use the New China Tea Room, in Cholon. Your contact is Mr. Long the owner and here is the phone number. Your code word for contact is you want to *order India tea*." "Got it?"

"Got it. What about the Duc Phan taxi? Do I still use it?" I asked.

"Yes. I don't want you using a regular taxi to make pick-ups and going to the plantation. Here's the expense money." Jack pushed a couple of envelopes in my direction then continued. "Forette's money has been deposited as usual. Whitley I want you to keep a sharp eye. Be aware of things around you."

"Like what specifically?"

"You know, check to see if you are being followed, strange or unusual occurrences, new people wanting to be your friend or people asking too many questions, things like that."

"Yes sir, I'll keep my eyes open." I said and knew immediately I should have told Jack about the girl at the hotel. But knowing the way Jack handles things, like the

Major and his girlfriend, I wanted to be sure in my own mind before I said anything.

"Stay in town and I'll have your next assignment in a couple of days. In fact, check in day after tomorrow and I'll have it ready for you."

"Yes sir. Day after tomorrow." I said and left the Embassy and headed to the hotel.

A hot shower and a nap with the air conditioner running was just the thing I needed. I didn't wake up until Charlie entered the room.

"Hey Charlie, let me know when you're ready and I'll go down to dinner with you."

"Not tonight pal. I have a date, and from what I understand so do you." Was Charlie's reply.

"What do you mean?"

"Ling is down stairs in the bar waiting for you."

"I wonder how the hell she even knows I'm in town, and who do you have a date with?

"A *round eye* with the State Department, she is over here with a group on a fact finding trip, and I am her official escort."

"Well, nice work if you can get it. What does she look like?"

"Very, very nice." Charlie said doing an hour glass figure with his hands.

"That's why they stuck her with you."

"What do you mean?"

"She is probably some married big shot's mistress and they figured she would be safe with a nerd like you."

"Yeah, very funny. You better get dressed or Ling might find someone else to take her out."

Charlie was still in the shower when I left to go down stairs. Sure enough, Ling was at the bar giving the cold shoulder to a couple of journalist trying to hit on her.

"See, I told you I was waiting for someone." She said to the two guys and they gave up and went back to their table.

"Hi. Waiting for me?" I asked, just to make sure.

"Thank you, some of these men get bothersome when they have too much to drink." She smiled then continued. "I have been waiting for you."

"Yeah, I wanted to ask you about that. Just how did you know I was back in Saigon?"

"Your roommate told me you were back."

I knew that was a lie, because Charlie had no idea I was back until he walked into the room. I wondered why she would lie about something so stupid. She could have said that she seen me on the street, and I would have never known the difference. My problem is not the lie, but why she would lie. Maybe, I thought, I should have told Roark about her.

We had drinks at the bar then went to dinner at the same restaurant as before. If only the girl didn't ask so many questions. She really gave herself away over dinner when she asked me why I was at the Embassy today. Even if she had been coming to the hotel bar every night looking for me and lied because she was too embarrassed to admit it, there was absolutely no way she could have known I was at the Embassy. I told her I work at the VE-AD compound and never said anything about the Embassy.

We closed the restaurant and went next door to her apartment. Ling may be a liar but her charms are beyond resisting. The next morning, as before, she left before me and I made my way back to my hotel.

I slept until noon then went downstairs for lunch and got into a card game. As promised Ling showed up about 3pm and took me to a movie. It was one of those Ballywood Indian movies with a lot of fight scenes, about a young nobody in love with the Raja's daughter in Hindi with Chinese and Vietnamese subtitles. Ling explained what was going on, but it didn't take much to follow the plot. If you have seen one of those movies you have seen them all. After the movie she took me to the river and we ate dinner on one of those floating restaurants, then back to my hotel for drinks. When I told her I would be leaving again, she started to pout when I couldn't tell her when I would be back. If I didn't know better, I think Ling really likes me, or maybe she is just good at pushing my ego button. Just as well, we couldn't have spent the night together anyway because of old Mother Nature. I walked her back to her apartment and we had a long kiss goodnight.

CHAPTER 16

The General

The next morning I walked down to the Embassy to pick up our next assignments. As soon as I walked in Jack started in on me about why I didn't tell him about Ling. He was really pissed. Madder than I have ever seen him.

"That is just the kind of stuff I was telling you about. Someone new taking an interest in you. Asking a lot of questions. You better wise up, you can get yourself killed in this business and take others with you. Now tell me everything."

So I started at the beginning and told him everything about Ling. He said he would check into it. I picked up the large sealed envelope with the next assignment in it and left feeling like a fool. Something inside me told me Jack was right and I should have told him to start with.

There was no pick-up at the New China Tea Room so I took the Duc Phan taxi directly back to the plantation. That night after dinner we retired to the office so Alain could read over the file on the next job. While Alain was going through the file, I asked Muesell why Brian DeKemp and Sig Borland were not in the room. Muesell didn't answer but Alain did.

"With the last job, they have enough money to go home to South Africa." Alain said as he looked over the top of the folder he was holding.

"I think Brian wants to get his sister away from you." Muesell added then continued. "You know, he doesn't like you very much."

"They were only here until they got enough money to return home. That's all." Alain said then continued reading.

Finally Alain put the file down and poured himself a glass of cognac.

"With Sig and Brian gone, won't that leave us short handed?" I asked.

"We still have Xu Tan and Delbert if need be." Muesell said.

"Our next target is a General. The Military Commander of Duong Sao Provence. This one may be very difficult. Muesell take Xu Tan and go up to Tinh

Binh Duong for a couple of days and check things out." Alain said as he slid the file over to Muesell to look at.

I told Alain about the possible compromise and gave him the code words and the phone number for the New China Tea Room.

"Duke huh, like John Wayne." Alain said then wrote the phone number and the words India Tea in his directory. As our custom, Muesell poured each of us some cognac, we drank it and called it a night.

The next day Muesell and Xu Tan took the Renault and left the plantation. While I was looking for an opportunity to speak with Karen about her leaving, I overheard Alain talking with Brian and Sig trying to persuade them into staying at least for one more job. His efforts were fruitless, Brian DeKemp insisted it was time for them to go while they had a chance. I think the last job, the Major and his girlfriend, had gotten to Brian, and he had his mind made up to take the money he had already made and get out of Vietnam. Where Brian goes Sig goes.

I finally got a chance to talk with Karen and she seemed happy that they were leaving. So it was nice while it lasted, but like all good things it has to come to an end. She also told me that since Muesell was gone she would try and slip over to my room tonight if I wanted her to. Of course I told her yes.

At dinner that night Brian informed everyone that the Australian Consuls' office in Saigon had contacted the South African Embassy in Singapore and had arranged the exit permits with the Vietnamese government. Alain said he would be driving them to Saigon tomorrow to catch their flight.

That night I joined the men after dinner and had a few drinks. Sig Borland told us the story of their escape from the Khmer Rouge and traveling down the Mekong river to Vietnam. They were a close pair, Sig and Brian, and I could see Sig as a paid killer he's the kind of guy who is up for anything. Brian, on the other hand, was the cautious one always questioning everything and used to being the boss not just one of the guys. Maybe Alain was starting to wear on him, or maybe it was the up close and personal killing he had to do. What ever the reason for leaving, they would be on their way back to South Africa tomorrow.

"Some die and some are born." I said then continued to tell them about the time the unit I was with sweeping a village that had just been bombed due to poor intelligence. The Medics were busy tending some seriously wounded villagers, and it fell to me to help deliver a baby. "The girl was scared as hell and so was I, but nature took its course, and I pulled out a very angry baby boy."

"I would be angry too, if I were born in the middle of a war." Sig Borland said, then continued. "I'll be glad to be rid of Vietnam."

The drinks, a hot shower and no snoring coming from the next bed, and I fell asleep. Something woke me and I opened my eyes to see Karen coming in the room. She turned off the bedside lamp and I could see her silhouetted in the soft moonlight coming through the French doors. She undressed and joined me to say her goodbye, and a sweeter goodbye was never spoken without words.

The next few days were quiet and the plantation seemed almost empty with Brian, Karen and Sig gone, and Muesell still off doing his surveillance work with Xu Tan. I spent the mornings in the office reading. Delbert was too busy with plantation operations to be of any company. The afternoons I spent in philosophical conversations with Cia, who has the typical oriental point of view. *If things are meant to change, they will, eventually. So why get into a rush trying to change them.* Alain spent the days with the workers and only came to the house for meals. She was not anti-American, but held the view that the country would be better off without them.

After three days Muesell and Xu Tan returned, and after dinner I joined them and Alain in the office to hear their report.

"The problem is that he very rarely leaves the compound where his villa is located. All staff meetings are conducted there, and the place is fortified. Besides his twelve man personal bodyguard, there is a Company of ARVN quartered at the compound. He doesn't have to go out for anything, his mistress even lives there as a second wife. He has tutors come in for the children, he has fourteen altogether, five living there. Apparently when they are old enough, the children are shipped off to boarding schools. His principal wife has been ill for a long time and has her own Doctor who visits daily." Muesell paused then continued. "Well there it is. I don't think it can be done."

Alain thought for a moment as he studied the aerial photo of the compound, then asked. "You said he rarely leaves." "What would draw him out?"

"An inspection of his units, or maybe a trip to Saigon if he is summoned by the General Staff, or to attend a Presidential function, other than that, only when he decides to." Muesell said.

"So if we can arrange a trip to Saigon for the General, we can ambush him." Alain asked.

"Sure, no problem, but you know he will have bodyguards with him. We'll have to kill them all." Muesell replied.

"If we know when he is leaving and where he is going." I interjected.

"That is something you can ask Duke if he can arrange." Alain was talking to me, then he continued. "Now tell me, who visits the villa on a regular basis?"

"The Doctor, the teacher, an old Buddhist Priest, Staff Officers in the mornings, sometimes one or two in the afternoon. Now that is the villa, people are going in and out of the compound all day long. The cook goes to market every morning after breakfast, he is driven by one of the bodyguards. That's it, the General doesn't leave. We didn't even see him while we were there."

"How do you even know he is there?" Alain asked.

"The girl. Oh, I forgot to tell you about the girl. Xu Tan found a girl who used to be one of the servants, she complained that she was raped by two of the soldiers and was fired. That's where we got the information for this." Muesell pulled a folded piece of paper from his pocket. "It is a detailed map of the compound and villa."

"We can use this, I hope you paid her well. We don't want her talking to anyone else, telling them you were asking questions about the General."

Xu Tan spoke up this time in Vietnamese.

"What did he say just now?" I asked.

"He said, she won't talk anymore, to anyone." Alain replied.

"That's what I thought he said." I remarked and thought this sure is a blood thirsty bunch. I justified it in my mind that they did what they did to protect the operation.

"Like I said, I'm not sure this can be done." Muesell said.

"Oh, it can and will be done, even if we have to go in hard. We will need more men to do it that way, but it is a last resort. For now I want you and Xu Tan to go back for two more days, maybe there is something you missed, and Whitley you better head to Saigon and talk to Duke. Find out about having the General summoned to Saigon, if not, tell him this is going to cost more. A lot more, if we have to have more men."

With that the meeting was over and we all left Alain alone to think and study the paperwork some more.

The next morning Alain drove me back to Saigon and I briefed Roark upon arrival.

Yeah, I know this is going to be a hard one. The surveillance and briefing reports from the other team, pretty much say the same thing." Roark said.

"So we're not the first team to draw this one. They didn't do anything to compromise the mission. Did they?"

"No. Their idea was to use a sniper, but there is no vantage point that looks down into the compound except up a utility poll, and they couldn't see into the villa its self, and how long can you keep a man up a poll. Next they put the shooter back up the poll and blew up a car in front of the gate, hoping that bring the General out, but it didn't, so I had them scrap the job. Now as far as getting the General summoned to Saigon, we can't go through the Palace. The man we would have to go to is also under suspicion, but, I may be able to do something else. I'll let you know late tomorrow, maybe a Embassy function or something." Jack got up from his desk and got his suit jacket off the coat rack then continued. "Right now, I have a meeting so I'll see you tomorrow afternoon."

At he hotel, I peeked into the bar to see if Ling was there, before going up to the room. Ling wasn't there so I stretched out on the bed and figured I would go down later. I was still stretched out when Charlie came in.

"So how was your date, Lover Boy?" I asked, kidding him a little.

"It was OK I guess, but kind of like taking your own sister to the prom."

"Say what?"

"Yeah, close enough to smell, but not to taste. You were right, she is the girlfriend of some Congressman. Just along for the ride and his pleasure."

"Oh man, you know I was just kidding about what I said the other night."

"Yeah I know, but that doesn't change the fact that you nailed on the head."

"Talking about nailing something, you didn't see Ling downstairs. Did you?"

"No. I haven't seen Ling since the last time you were in and ran in to her in the lobby."

"Let me ask you something. That day, did you tell her I was here?"

"I told her I thought you were, because I saw you at the Embassy." "Why?"

"Nothing. Don't worry about it. I was just trying to figure out how she knew I was at the Embassy that day."

"Did I do something wrong?"

"No, like I said don't worry about it. It was just something she said. That's all."

Well I was relieved. I was wrong about Ling, she wasn't lying to me. It was just like she said. Charlie told her I was in Saigon because he saw me at the Embassy.

I was glad and looking forward to seeing Ling. I got up and hit the shower.

Ling still wasn't downstairs so I started without her. I was on my third drink and still no Ling. I was getting hungry so I decided to walk down to the restaurant next to her place, but by this time it was getting close to curfew so I stayed and just had a hamburger and a few more drinks. It was after midnight so there was no chance Ling was coming tonight so I went back upstairs and called it a night.

The next day I decided to walk down to Ling's hotel since I didn't have to see Roark until this afternoon. I wrote a note and asked the man at the desk to give it to her when she came in. The man said he would, but he also said that he hadn't seen her in few days and she might be out of town. Ling hadn't said anything about going out of town the last time I talked with her, but that's been a couple of days ago. I walked back to my hotel and had lunch then walked to the Embassy to see Roark.

Jack wasn't in his office when I got there so I went to the cafeteria for a cup of coffee. While there, Jack came in and sat down at the same table.

"Well I've got some good news and some bad news. Come on up to the office when you finish your coffee."

"I'm finished. I was just waiting for you anyway." I told him and followed him back up the stairs to the first floor. Inside the office he continued.

"Like I said, good news and bad news. The bad news is that there is no way to get him summoned to Saigon.

The good news is I arranged for the ARVN Battalion that has the Company quartered at the General's compound to be in support of an upcoming operation, so you have a window of about six days when the only people at the compound will be the General and his family, his personal bodyguard and household staff. Tell Forette to hire who ever he needs, we have received more intelligence that the General is a major player for the north and they are planning some assassinations of their own. This job has got to be done what ever it takes, but it can't look like we did it." Roark paused and went to his safe to open it. He tossed a package to me then continued. "Here's ten thousand in cash and there will be a bonus of fifteen thousand put in the bank when the job is done." "Any questions?"

"Just one that comes to mind. How in the hell to we make an operation of this size look like the Viet Cong did it?"

"You kill everyone inside the compound. Everyone knows that the Americans don't operate like that. Besides, you can't leave any witnesses behind to tell a different story anyway. Tell Forette that I am sending a couple of my people to help out and they will be bringing some equipment and some stuff our magic boys are working on, but it is his operation."

Well I had my marching orders so I returned to the plantation to relay the information to Alain. We had about ten days to plan and execute the operation with an outside window of fifteen days. Alain went to work immediately to find more manpower. It is not like you can go to the phone book and look up mercenaries, but

Alain has lived in this country long enough to have the contacts.

Muesell and Xu Tan returned the following day with some new information. They found a metal door in the back wall that was locked with a chain. This door didn't show up on any of the aerial photographs or on any of the intelligence reports and apparently not in use because of the weeds that have grown up in front of it. Other than the door there wasn't any new information. Muesell was sent out again immediately to talk to some of Alain's contacts. The same day Delbert Foo left on an extended business trip, taking the boy that had been taken and released by the VC with him. I assumed it was to prevent the local VC from getting wind that something big was going on at the plantation.

Two days later the two men, that Jack had sent, showed up at the plantation. I don't think that Alain was happy with the men, but being short of man power, he didn't complain too much. They brought with them some captured North Vietnamese Army equipment, including several AK 47 assault rifles with bandoleers and satchel charges commonly used by Viet Cong sappers. They also had in there possession printed flyers accusing the General of being a traitor to the National Liberation Front (Viet Cong) by stealing money that was meant to go north. The two guys looked like they were Special Forces or ex-Special Forces working as CIA operators. We referred to them as Blue and Green. They were both Asian, probably of Pilipino descent, and spoke Vietnamese fluently, but I could tell they were American by the way they acted and so could Alain. The two spent hours with Alain going over different plans. Other than that and meals they kept to themselves on the other side of the gardens in the room Sig Borland and Brian DeKemp had occupied.

The nights were boring with no midnight visits with Karen. I spent them thinking of Karen and Ling, and hoping I would see Ling on my next visit to Saigon. I read the paperback books I had with me at least twice each. Anything to keep my mind off the upcoming mission.

Late the next evening Muesell returned with two men and one to follow the next day. One of the guys was also a ex-Legionnaire, a Malaysian who had been a Sergeant and served with Alain and Muesell. The second man was a Vietnamese-Chinese, who best I can figure is some kind of gangster from Cholon called Mongol. The next day the third man arrived, a big German named Fritz, also an ex-Legionnaire.

So that is it, the nine of us. Blue and Green, Sergeant Tang, Mongol, Fritz, Xu Tan, Alain, Muesell, and me. I hope there is still nine of us when the mission is over.

CHAPTER 17

"Cry Havoc And Let Slip
The Dogs Of War"

The plan was done and we went over it, and over it, and over it. We were all military men except Mongol and Xu Tan. There was no doubt in Alain's mind that we would get the job done. Every last detail that could be planed for was planed for. Normally some of the bodyguards would be off on Saturday night and some more on Sunday night, but with the ARVN soldiers gone from the compound we couldn't count on any of the bodyguards being off so we planned for all twelve of them being there. The operation was set for Sunday night, right in the middle of our window. The General, his mistress, wife, four live in servants including the cook, the children, and twelve bodyguards, we counted on nineteen adults being in the compound. We had plenty of fire power, provided we didn't miss anything. We were out numbered two to one, but we had surprise on our side.

Mongol, through his contacts, found us a building that backed onto the same alley that ran behind the compound. The alley wasn't wide enough for vehicles, not much more than a foot path, so we could count on it being empty at 0300 hours, kick off time.

Early Saturday morning we headed to Tinh Binh Duong in Duong Sao Provence. We packed all nine of us and our equipment into both cars. It was a tight fit and an uncomfortable ride. When we got there we started moving equipment and men, a couple at a time, into the building we were going to use as a staging area. When we were finished, we parked both cars on the street in front of the building. From the back of the building to the rear gate of the compound was about two hundred yards down the alley. At 1400 hours, Alain sent Xu Tan down the alley with a can of penetrating oil to soak the hinges on the gate. Now there is nothing to do except check our weapons and wait.

When Xu Tan returned, he and Sergeant Tang broke out the Chinese version of a Coleman stove and started cooking our dinner. While waiting for dinner Blue and Green got into their packs and pitched a couple of C-ration meals over to Sergeant Tang then started to clean their weapons. When they pulled a couple of strange looking pistols out and started breaking them down, I asked.

"What kind of guns are those?"

"This, my friend, is the Mk 22 Hush Puppy with silencer and sub sonic 9mm ammo." Blue said as he held one up.

"Why do they call it a Hush Puppy?" I asked.

Green spoke up and said. "To take care of any guard dogs, quietly." "Understand?"

"Yep, got it." I said as I was even more convinced that these two are either Army Special Forces or Navy Seals.

After a meal of dried fish with fish sauce, Chinese noodle soup and fried rice made with the addition of pork and chicken from the C-rations, every one settled down to get a few hours sleep before the operation.

At 1100 hours, Alain woke me to take my turn at guard. I got a cup of coffee and tried hard to take my mind off the operation. I looked around the large room, it wasn't much, just concrete block walls and concrete floor, a water faucet coming out of the wall with a bucket on the floor underneath, and a sewer pipe flush with the floor in one corner for a toilet. At midnight I fixed a coffee and woke Fritz up to take his turn on guard. Fritz sat up and I handed him his coffee. He spoke French, some Vietnamese and of course German. I asked him, in German, how he liked it when he was in the Legion.

"It is a hard life for all, but a good life for some. Me, I liked the Legion."

"Why did you leave the Legion if you liked it so much?" I asked him.

"For me it was simple. I like Vietnam and the people and I didn't want to go back to the desert in Cameroon, which is where they were going to send me if I signed up again. For me I think six years was enough."

Fritz got up to move around and I laid back down and dozed off. At 0200 hours, Alain got everyone up to start getting ready. Alain, Sergeant Tang, Xu Tan and Mongol dressed in black Viet Cong style PJs and web gear. Muesell, Fritz and I dressed in black fatigues, and Blue and Green wearing black fatigue pants with black pull-over long sleeve shirts and watch caps. As we were blacking our faces, Alain went over the plans one more time. After cutting the chain on the back gate with bolt cutters, hoping that the oil on the hinges did its job, Blue, Green, Muesell and I would go after the guards in the barracks. Fritz would remain in the courtyard as back up. Alain, Sergeant Tang, Xu Tan, and Mongol would move to the house.

Equipment check. We all carried AK 47s with extra magazines. Blue and Green had their Mk22s and the printed flyers that we would leave behind, Muesell and Alain had our other two pistols with silencers, I had my 45 and two grenades, Fritz and Sergeant Tang were carrying satchel charges in case we need them. Mongol and Xu Tan, instead of side arms, were carrying machetes, Xu Tan also had carried the bolt cutters.

Ready to go now, Sergeant Tang offered a salute saying.

"Vive la mort." followed by Muesell, who said.

"vive la guerre." Then the rest joined in, led by Alain.

"vive le sacre mercenaire." (*Long live death, long live war, long live the cursed mercenary.*)

0245 hours we exited the front door two at a time and headed to the back of the building. It was dark, but enough light to see. Everything was deathly quite only an occasional dog barking somewhere in the distance. We made our way down the alley toward the back of the compound. The phone lines came in from the street in front of the compound so we couldn't risk cutting them, so it was key that we got inside without letting ourselves be known. Xu Tan cut the chain, and slowly, Alain pulled on the gate. The oil had worked, the gate opened, with resistance, but quietly enough that it wouldn't be heard. We can't see the front gate, because there is a shed that is used for a garage is in the way. We can see the guard barracks from where we are, just past the apparently empty and completely dark ARVN building, but no guards in sight.

Alain motioned for us to remain where we are, then went to the other end of the building. A few seconds later he returned.

"There is one guard in front of the house sitting on the steps leaning on his rifle, he looks like he is half asleep. There are two guards at the main gate, they are smoking and talking." Alain whispered, then continued. "Get into position. When you take out the guards at the front gate, I'll take out the one in front of the house." Alain said as he tapped Blue on the shoulder.

We then split up. Blue, Green, Muesell and I moved along the back wall to the left staying in the shadows until it was safe to cross to the edge of the barracks. Alain, Mongol, Xu Tan, Fritz and Sergeant Tang went to the right behind the shed.

The overhang that runs along the front of the guard barracks gave us plenty of shadow to make it up to the door of the body guard's hut. Blue looked inside the door and saw no movement, only bunks and men sleeping. Blue motioned for me and Muesell to stay put and he and Green continued to move to the end of the building closer to the guards at the main gate. I glanced across the courtyard and could barely make out Alain and the other group, they were almost on the single guard.

Two pops, then two more in rapid succession and the gate guards are down. Across the way and one shot to the head of the third guard and he is down. Muesell and I are ready to enter the guard barracks as we are rejoined by Blue and Green. A look inside confirms that the rest of the guards are still asleep. We enter the building at the same time as Alain and his group enter the house. In the courtyard there is someone yelling in Vietnamese then shots from an AK 47 and the yelling stops.

Well no surprise now, we immediately opened up on the sleeping guards killing them all. Blue told me and Muesell to search the rest of the building, then he and Green left to join the other group in the house. We found the house boy huddled in the corner of the kitchen.

Muesell shot him. The rest of the building was clear. As we exited we could see Blue, Green and Fritz all shooting up at the second floor of the ARVN building, and we could hear gun fire coming from the house. Muesell and I ran to the front door of the ARVN building and entered, we could hear a gun being fired from the second floor. We worked our way up the stairs and found one man in his underwear shooting into the courtyard from one of the windows. I pulled the pin on a grenade and rolled it in his direction and Muesell and I ran half way back down the stairs. When the grenade went off we returned to find the man dead and continued to clear the rest of the building.

Not finding anyone else in the ARVN building we exited to find Fritz and Green throwing the flyers into the air, and the rest of the crew exiting the house. We all made our way to the back gate. We passed a dead guard in the courtyard on the way, and my heart was beating ninety miles an hour. Muesell pushed the metal gate shut and we made our way back down the alley, quietly, but quickly. All hell was breaking loose all around us. Dogs were barking, lights were coming on and we could hear sirens coming down the main street. It seemed like it took for ever, but we finally made it to the back of our building without being noticed.

We all immediately changed back into our street clothes, with no one saying a word. I looked at my watch and was dumbfounded to realize it was only 0315 hours. It had only been 30 minutes since we left our building and arrived back. We were only in the compound about twelve or thirteen minutes and it seemed like an eternity.

Alain wanted to gather all the AK 47 rifles, NVA and Viet Cong gear, and hide them on the roof in case the buildings in the area were searched. Mongol said no one would do a house to house search, there weren't enough police in this town to do it and most of the ARVN soldiers were away on a operation. Blue agreed with Mongol and said that since we were stuck here until tomorrow we should keep the arms and ammo ready just as a back up. Alain relented and we all settled down to get some rest and wait to see what tomorrow would bring. I finally fell asleep amid the sound of sirens in the distance and going over the details of the last half hour in my mind.

CHAPTER 18

The Last Waltz

The next day, Alain told Mongol to gather up all the Viet Cong and NVA gear, and five of the AK 47s and get rid of them. We couldn't have any incriminating evidence with us on the way back to Saigon. While waiting for Sergeant Tang and Mongol to get back, we went over the details of the night before. The things that went wrong were missing the guard in the outside latrine, and not knowing there was a soldier left behind in the ARVN building. Either of those mistakes could have cost us major causalities. We were damn lucky.

I heard Alain say that there were no survivors left behind, but it didn't dawn on me until now, that meant the children were also killed. A sick feeling suddenly overwhelmed my entire body and I started vomiting violently. So violently that I thought my knees were going to buckle, but they held. Luckily I was close the hole in the floor used for a latrine. I steadied my self by propping my self up with a hand on the wall, still not sure I wasn't going to end up in a crumpled heap on the floor.

"I told you not to eat that fish sauce." Fritz said to me in German as he pitched a pan of water on the floor to wash everything down the hole in the floor.

"Bad noodles." I replied still steadying myself with a hand on the wall.

As soon as Mongol and Sergeant Tang got back, Xu Tan got busy with a wide roll of red reflective tape putting red crosses on the doors of the cars. Alain passed out Red Cross arm bands for everyone, and Alain, Muesell and I clipped on our Red Cross ID cards.

We were leaving with less equipment than we came with, but it was still crowded. We went through two check points on the way to Saigon. We slowed down and were waived through the first. At the second we were only stopped briefly. When the guard stepped back and waived Alain in the first car through, Muesell didn't even stop for him, he just stayed right on Alain's back bumper.

It was noon when we arrived back at the plantation and we all sat down to the meal that had been prepared. Finally the air lightened and all the ex-legionnaires were joking with each other. Nothing else was said about the mission. I had trouble sleeping that night thinking about the children, the women, and the servants being killed. I was glad I was not in the group that went into the house and the only person I killed was with a grenade. At least he was a soldier, even if he was an ARVN, one of our allies.

The next day I left the plantation with Green and Blue. Alain as usual dropped us off in Cholon. Green and Blue headed to a bar and I took a taxi to the Embassy to give my after action report to Jack Roark.

"Whitley, come on in and have a seat."

I did, and waited for Jack to get off the phone. I lit a smoke while I waited. Finally Jack hung up the phone and said.

"Well tell me how it went."

"Mission was accomplished, the General is dead and no causalities on our side. I don't know if the locals bought the bit about it being done by the Viet Cong or not, but we left the leaflets behind." I told him as I returned all the paper work he had given me on the assignment.

"Leaflets?" "Oh yes, the leaflets. Oh well, we'll know in a day or two how that works out. What happened to the two men I sent?"

"The two Americans. The last time I saw them was about forty minutes ago headed into a bar in Cholon."

"Let's get one thing straight. There were no other Americans on this mission." "Do you understand. Even if Colonel Augden asks, the only American remotely involved with this operation was you."

"Yes sir." I replied, not really understanding why he was so insistent about it.

Jack went to his safe and pulled out a file and a letter size envelope stuffed until it was almost an inch thick and taped with brown postal tape. He tossed me the envelope and said.

"This is for Forette." Then sat back down at his desk and opened the file. "When you get back to the plantation tomorrow, tell Forette I'll be sending a replacement for you. I want you to pack your gear and come back to Saigon."

"Have I done something wrong?" I asked.

"No. We finally got into the safes at the bar and the Major's girlfriend's house. We found among the documents some more photographs of you and some other personnel. So it's time for you to move on. That's all."

"What do I do when I get back?"

"Report in to Colonel Augden. You are his man." "And Whitley, you've done a good job. It's for your own protection, as well as others."

"I understand." I said as I got up to leave.

I wasn't disappointed that I was being pulled out, but I was more than a little anxious about what my next assignment would be. Anyway I put it out of my mind for now, because I wanted to get to the hotel. I was looking forward to seeing Ling again.

At the hotel, I checked inside the bar for Ling before going upstairs to the room. She wasn't there and Charlie wasn't back from the office yet. I hit the shower then lay on the bed to catch a nap before what I was hoping was to be a long night.

I awoke to Charlie coming in. It was 1600 hours and I had slept longer than I had planed. While shaving I asked Charlie.

"You didn't notice Ling down stairs. Did you?"

"Come to think about it, it has been a week or so since I've seen her. I thought you two might be off on a pre-honeymoon." Charlie said then laughed at his own attempt at humor.

"No. In fact, I didn't even get to see her the last time I was in. The desk man at her hotel said he thought she might be out of town."

"You'll probably catch up to her tonight." "Are you about done in there? I need a shower."

"Yeah, no problem. It's all yours." I said as I splashed, then wiped the remaining soap off my face. A little Old Spice and I was ready to go.

Ling was still not in the bar, so I decided to walk the three blocks to her hotel and see if I could catch her in. I went in through the back and up the stairs. I knocked on her door, but there was no answer so I went down to talk to the man at the front desk.

"Miss Ling no here. She never come back." He said in his broken English.

"What do you mean? She never came back. She still lives here, doesn't she?"

"No Sir, she no come back."

"She didn't come back from where?" I asked, not sure if I was making myself clear.

"I don't know Sir. One day she leave and she no come back."

"Are her things still in the room?"

"No Sir, Vietnam man and Police come, they show me picture of Miss Ling and ask me if it her." "I tell them yes and they take all. Man say she no come back." He said apologetically, then continued. "I'm sorry Sir, I think she go see ancestors."

"You mean, you think she is dead."

"Yes Sir, I think it true." He said as he fumbled around with something behind the desk and came up with a business card and showed it to me.

I couldn't read the card so I asked him what it said. He said it was the card of Captain Hap Vien Lau of the Saigon District Police. I wrote down the name, thanked him and left.

My initial instinct was to go find this Police Captain and see if he could give me any more information. After thinking about it, considering my own situation, and not knowing the circumstances of her death, I figured I had better stay clear of the police. The police were sure to ask questions that I couldn't answer and that would only make me a suspect if she was murdered and not involved in an accident of some kind. It is quite possible that Jack Roark had her killed to eliminate a security risk, real or not, I thought. It is also possible that what ever happened to her had nothing what-so-ever to do with me. To many things running around in my mind, I decided to go back to the hotel and get drunk and try to quiet my mind.

The next morning I had a hangover, but not as bad as I thought it would be. A long shower and I was feeling better, a little food and I would be good-to-go. After getting something to eat I walked back to the Embassy to catch my usual taxi back to the plantation. On the ride, I thought more and more about how angry Jack was when he found out about the girl. I just about convinced myself that he was responsible for Ling's death. Maybe he was justified, I just don't know. She did latch on to me out of the blue, and she did ask a lot of questions. Maybe I let my own vanity blind me to what she was up to, maybe, and maybe it was just what it was, a man and a woman.

This would be my last night at the plantation. I had given Alain his money and told him I was being replaced and briefed him on the other changes. We put away almost a half bottle of cognac while we were talking about what had gone on while I was with them.

I had about three hours before dinner so I decided to lay down for awhile. It was time for me to put this stuff out of my mind, it was over for me now and I could go back to just being a soldier. When I think about what we have done, I just had to tell myself it was justified in the larger scheme of things. A soldier killing in combat is one thing, but the work I have been doing just didn't feel like the same thing. I felt dirty.

While I was asleep my replacement had arrived. Another young Sergeant I assumed, I hoped he was more suited for this kind work than me. It is not that I didn't do my job well, I did, I just don't have the stomach for it. Alain introduced Adam Shurgelt at dinner as my replacement. Everyone at the table toasted Adam on his arrival and me on my departure.

Adam came to my room that night. He had a million questions, some I answered but most I was vague about and just explained that past operations were classified. I gave him the run down on the people at the plantation and that's about it. He told me he had been stuck in a office at COORDS since he arrived in-country about six months ago, and was looking forward to getting out in the field. I told him that this wasn't really the *field,* but it would be different than working in an office.

CHAPTER 19

Jack Gets One More

The next morning I packed my gear and was surprised to find it was Muesell who was going to give me a ride back to Saigon. He didn't have much to say on the hot ride, but when he pulled over to the side of the road in Cholon he turned to me and said.

"You know, I have changed my mind. When you first arrived, I didn't think too much of you, but I was wrong." he paused for a moment then continued. "You have the heart of a lion, stay safe my friend." Muesell said as he offered to shake hands.

I shook hands with Muesell, got my gear and exited the vehicle. I watched Muesell pull off then caught a taxi and headed to the hotel to drop my bag off, then took another taxi to the VE-AD compound.

At the compound I knocked on Colonel Augden's door. "Come on in." came the reply.

"Sergeant Whitley have a seat. I'll be with you in just a minute." Augden said as he continued with his phone call.

When he hung up the phone he sat back in his chair for a moment before he started talking. "I talked with Roark and he replaced you because you were getting too involved with the operations, and he was getting worried about your safety." "Did you know that?"

"No Sir. Jack told me that it was because more photographs of me had turned up."

"Well, I'm sure that was part of it too. Anyway, I was getting ready to send you on R&R but Roark says he has one more job for you." "How would you like about ten days in the states on us?"

"Yes Sir, sounds good to me, what am I going to be doing?"

"Don't know exactly, but when you get back I'm sending you back to the Army with your choice of assignments." "Is that OK with you?"

"Yes Sir."

"OK then, don't check-out of the hotel until you get back from your assignment, and check-out with Operation before you go see what Roark wants."

I stood and saluted, even though we were both in civilian clothes. At Operations I saw Big M and turned-in my Department of Defense, VE-AD, and Red Cross ID card and in return got my Army ID and dog tags back. Next stop, back to the Embassy to find out what Jack wants.

At the Embassy, Jack filled me in on my assignment and it was a give-me. All I had to do was to fly to Washington DC and pick up a package and return it to Jack, and I had ten days to do it in. On the way over, I had decided not to say anything to Jack about Ling. As it has before, my mouth overloaded my ass and I asked Jack if he had anything to do with Ling's disappearance. I said *disappearance*, because I didn't want to accuse the man of murder even though we both knew he was quite capable of ordering it. Jack looked up from behind his desk and said "No." That's it, just no. He handed me a set of Joint State Department and Department of the Army travel orders and a $950 voucher, that I cashed at the finance cage on the first floor, for expense money, he then sent me to Embassy security to have Classified Courier credentials made. At the Embassy travel office I booked a flight to Hawaii leaving Tan San Nhut air field at 1400 hours the next day. My orders said I was going to the Pentagon, but I was actually headed to Fort Detrick, Maryland to pick up a package from an Army Doctor working there. Anything to do with Jack Roark had the usual cloak-and-dagger to go along with it, code words, recognition signs, counter signs, and the like. I was to check-in to a motel close by and call the Doctor at home that night, to make arrangements for an eyeball to eyeball first, then the Doctor would pass me the package later at the motel. I think Jack goes a little overboard with all this clandestine bull, but Jack is the expert, supposedly, and I am the amateur. Like I said, this assignment is a give-me, so I'll follow my orders to the letter.

At the hotel, I had dinner and a couple of drinks at he bar in the restaurant then went up to the room. I was authorized to travel in civilian cloths, but didn't have anything suitable so I got into my duffel and pulled out a set of tans, the staff sergeant stripes on the sleeves were still new to me, because I haven't had much of a chance to wear them since I was promoted. I gave the uniform to the mama san at the end of the hall for her to steam and press and told her I needed the uniform back as soon as possible. I then went back to the room to get everything else ready for tomorrow. I had just dosed off when Charlie came into the room carrying my uniform.

"Man, I knew you were military." What's going on now?" He said as he offered me the uniform.

"Just hang it in the closet Charlie. Well you are going to lose a room mate."

"When are you going, tomorrow?"

"Yes and no. I'm leaving to go back to the states for a short R&R tomorrow, but I'll be back in a couple of weeks before heading out."

"Where are you going when you get back?"

"Don't know. I'll find out when I get back."

"So, you want to tell me what you have been doing? Some kind of Special Ops, I bet."

"You got some imagination Charlie. Nothing so exciting I'm afraid. Just been working on an agriculture study."

"An agriculture study. Bullshit, then why all the hush-hush?"

"Come on Charlie. I'm not the one who classifies this stuff. I'm just a peon doing my job. Now that the study is done, I'll be going back to the real Army. That's all."

"Bullshit. You're some kind of Agent man, you're probably not even in the Army, but if you don't want to tell me, you don't have to."

"Hey Charlie I have a 2:pm flight out of Tan San Nhut tomorrow, you think you can get a vehicle and give me a ride to the airport?"

"Sure, no problem, I'll pick you up a little after noon."

"Thanks pal."

Well Charlie showed up on time the next day and off to Hawaii I went. I got to skip customs with my classified courier ID and booked two nights in one of the beach front hotels. I had two days of nothing to do except lay on the beach in the day, drink tropical cocktails in the afternoons, and disco into the wee hours.

While in Hawaii I bought a sports coat, a couple pair of slacks and dress shirts, and other odds and ends. Two days later I caught a flight to SeaTac airport in Seattle with a connecting flight to Chicago where I changed planes for Louisville so I could spend a couple of days at home before going on to Washington DC. After my visit at home, I took a flight to DC where I rented a car and drove to Frederick Maryland and got a motel room on the highway leading to Fort Detrick.

That night I called my contact, a Doctor Blumenrich, and identified my self by asking if he attended Stanford. He replied correctly by saying, he only attended one year, then transferred to Marquette. Now I don't know if he ever went to Stanford or Marquette, all I know is that is what he was suppose to say. So we made arrangements to eat at the snack bar at Fort Detrick tomorrow at 1230 hours. I was to have a picture post card laying on the table in front of me so I would be recognized.

The next morning I ate breakfast at the local pancake house down the street from the motel. As I was paying my bill I picked a post card at random of the rack by the register, then back to the motel. At about a quarter till noon, I wrote the name, address of the motel, along with my room number on the card, then headed out to Fort Detrick.

The sign at the entrance read, "FORT DETRICK HOME OF THE UNITED STATES ARMY MEDICAL RESEARCH AND DEVELOPEMENT COMMAND, BIOLOGICAL WARFARE LABORATORIES". I waited my turn then pulled up to the guard.

"Good afternoon Sir. May I see your identification, please?"

I handed my Army ID to the officer then he continued.

"Is the vehicle registered to you Sergeant Whitley?" The guard asked as he handed my ID back.

"No. It's a rental."

"Do you have your rental agreement with you?"

"Why all the security, is something special going on?" I asked as I got the car papers out of the glove box for him.

"No sir, standard procedures. What is your purpose at Fort Detrick today Sergeant?"

Wow, I wasn't ready for that one, but I responded quickly, thinking back to my training on Operation Norseman, in Europe, *Keep it simple*. "I'm a Classified Courier, I just made a delivery to the Pentagon, and I'll be returning to Vietnam day after tomorrow." I said as I took my credentials out along with a copy of my orders I had folded up with them and showed them to the Guard."

He looked at my courier ID and read my orders then said. "Yes sir, but why are you at Fort Detrick?"

"Oh. Just meeting an old friend of mine for lunch while I'm in the area."

"OK Sergeant, keep this visitor pass on your dash, and you are required to be off post by 1600 hours." He said as he handed me the pass and waived me through.

I followed the sign to the Post Headquarters and according to my contact the snack bar would be just beyond. It was twelve thirty exactly as I parked and went in.

I went through the line and got some lunch then took a seat at one of the empty tables. I looked around the room and everyone seemed to be in conversation or eating. I took the post card out and placed it on the table while I was eating.

A few minutes passed when a full Colonel in tans with his lunch approached the table.

"Is this seat taken?"

"No, have a seat, please." I said, and knew this was my man. His name tag read, BLUMENRICH. His picture ID badge clipped to his pocket identified him as Doctor Blumenrich at the Biological Research Center, but he was wearing Chemical Corps brass instead of the Medical brass I had expected. He sat diagonally across from me and started eating.

"Are you Viking?" He said in a low voice without looking at me.

"The address and room number is on the card." I said in the same manner, then got up from the table leaving the card behind.

Approaching the main gate to leave I was waved over to an inspection area. I rolled down the window and handed the approaching guard the visitors pass. He took it then said.

"Exit the vehicle. Open the hood and trunk and wait in the area marked with the yellow paint."

I did as instructed as one guard looked in the car then the engine compartment and trunk while another guard walked around the car with a mirror on a long poll looking underneath the car. Now I have been in the Army for a while, and have never seen this kind of security getting on or off a military base. They seem to be more interested in what you are leaving with than what you are bringing in. After about a minute and a half one of the guards came over to me and said.

"OK sir, you're good to go. Have a nice day."

Back at the motel, I took a nap then watched a little TV waiting for the knock on the door. Finally, at six thirty the knock came. I opened the door and in came the Colonel, only this time he was in civilian clothes.

"Let's get this over with." He said as he sat the small package he was carrying down on the small table in the room, then sat down himself.

I joined him at the table and watched him open the package and take out a blue velvet box, that looked like a oversized ring box. The ring box had a Presidential Seal imprinted on the top. He opened the box and showed me a set of Presidential Seal cufflinks, the kind the President gives out as gifts to dignitaries at the White House.

"Do not, I repeat, do not touch these. Do not let anyone else touch them. They are activated by rubbing the surface. The agent is trans-dermal and lethal within 12 hours. Once activated the agent will only be active for about three or four hours" "Understand?"

I nodded in the affirmative while he closed the lid and placed the blue velvet box back in the package.

"Any questions?" He asked.

"No." I replied.

"I'm out of here." He said as he got up from the table and left the room. I heard his car start and pull off as I just sat there staring at the package.

The next morning I called the airport and made reservations for a non-stop to Seattle with a connecting flight to Hawaii. I had plenty of time to get to the airport so after checking-out of the motel I stopped by the local post office in Frederick. I bought a small roll of packing tape and a large padded envelope. I sealed the package and placed it in the envelope and wrote Official State Department documents on it and addressed it to the Cultural Attaché, American Embassy, Saigon RVN. I figured that even if I was searched the way the package was addressed along with my credentials and orders would keep it from being opened. This was totally unnecessary, I thought, but better safe than sorry.

A day and a half later, back in Hawaii, I checked-in to the Kale Hoa Hotel, the R&R Center, and made arrangements with the transportation office for space on a military charter headed to Vietnam in two days.

Arriving back in Vietnam I was greeted with the same stink and oppressive heat and humidity and I had been gone exactly ten days. My precautions with the package had been unnecessary after all, the only time I came close to a customs check was at Tan San Nhut and after showing my credentials I was waved through. I took the duty bus to Camp Alpha in Saigon, then took a taxi to the hotel where I dropped my bags in the room.

A shower and shave later and I was on my way to the Embassy to drop off my package. I met Jack coming down the main hallway and followed him back to his office.

"Have any problems?" Jack asked as he hung his coat up then sat down at his desk.

"No problems but, the contact did give some instructions." I said as I handed Jack the envelope.

"Like what?" He asked as he took the package out.

"Well he said don't touch the cufflinks --" Jack interrupted me.

"He showed them to you?"

"Yes. As I said, he said not to touch them, that the agent was trans-dermal and lethal within twelve hours then dissipates after four or five hours."

"Good, that is exactly what I was looking for." He said as he opened the blue velvet box to look at the cufflinks, then continued. "You forget you ever saw these, or anything to do with them." "Understand?"

"Understand." I said.

That was the last time I ever saw Jack Roark. I did hear from him again, but that is another story for another time. Colonel Augden was true to his word. I did get my choice of assignments, but I also incurred a six month extension on my tour.

I was off on a two week R&R to Australia before joining the Headquarters of the 9th Infantry Division at Dong Tam. While in Australia about 8 days later, I read in the newspapers that Vietnam's Minister of Finance along with his wife and one of his servants died un-expectantly of some unknown illness. I thought about Jack's package.

CHAPTER 20

Back In The Army Again

After my R&R, I was assigned to the headquarters of the 9th Infantry Division in Dong Tam. I was assigned to G3 Operations and worked in the Air Operations office for about a month to get the feel of things, then attached to the 2d Brigade headquarters as one of the three Air Liaison NCOs. My duty station was with the 3d of the 5th Cavalry. The Air Ops Officer, a Captain De Costa, and I worked out of the Battalion headquarters, but we spent most of our time with Delta Troop, the air support troop for the Battalion.

I got my wish. I was spending a lot of time flying. Either Captain D or I would fly on every combat operation, and both of us on big operations. For the first time in Vietnam

I actually loved my job. The living quarters aren't that great, no air conditioner or flush toilets, but I do love it. I don't pull any extra duties, or make formations like the other NCOs. I only answer to Captain D and he only answers to the Battalion Commander and the Assistant Chief of Staff for Operations at Division headquarters.

The 3d of the 5th Cavalry is tasked with supporting the 9th Infantry Division's Mobile Riverine Force, known as the MRF, a combined Army Navy force conducting combat operations on the Mekong and other rivers along with their tributaries and navigable canals. On joint operations the Cav with their armored personnel carriers, APCs, and additional troops delivered to the combat area by helicopters would provide the land part of the operation. The MRF would land amphibiously and provide the other half of the operation, like a big pincher designed to trap and destroy the enemy. Sometimes it works and sometimes it doesn't.

On one such operation we bit off more than we could chew. My job, as usual, was to coordinate the delivery of troops on the Huey Slicks and provide air support for the operation with the Huey gun ships, Hogs, as well as be the point of contact for other aircraft supporting the operation, including Army, Navy and Air Force planes, if any. Like I said, we bit off more than we could chew on this one.

We were deep in the delta, south of Can Tho. The enemy was suppose to be a small Viet Cong force of about forty to sixty men guarding an un-located supply dump. The MRF's mission was to come in the back door and surprise the Cong, engage and locate the supply dump. The engaging force of the MRF consisted of an entire Company of the 60th Infantry plus two squads of Rangers, approximately 120 soldiers and Navy gun boats preventing escape or reinforcement from the river. The Cav provided Bravo Troop's twelve APCs staged along the only road into the area, and air support from Delta Troop. We had four Hogs in the air that day, including the bird I was in. On stand-by we had four Cobra gun ships, and assigned dust-off (Med-Evac) crews from the aviation battalion.

The surprise turned out to be no surprise at all. While trying to land and debark the MRF come under heavy mortar and automatic weapons fire, forcing two of the three small transport boats to withdraw, the third took a direct mortar hit killing two of the soldiers and the boat Captain. This left about thirty-five men trapped and surrounded on the bank of the river. Four of the gunboats moved in close to the bank to give covering fire with their heavy machine guns. They too came under fire suffering some casualties. As we moved in with the birds we realized this was no small unit of sixty Cong.

The first thing we spotted was an entire mortar platoon in the open with six mortars firing on the men and boats along the bank. While I was calling the aviation unit for the Cobras we had on stand-by, and Delta Troop for more birds, I saw two of our Hogs drop down and decimate the mortar unit with rockets and heavy machine gun fire. There was about eighty or so Viet Cong that we could see and probably the same number, or more, that we couldn't see. We engaged as well, strafing what we could see with 50 cal. machine gun fire, and firing rockets into the tree line. It would be several minutes before the Cobras got in the area and the guys on the ground couldn't wait, so the Delta Troop pilots all got closer to the ground than they normally would have to get at the Cong. I had the extra radios in the bird I was in, and they were all on fire with traffic. The troops on the bank were calling for dust-off, two of our birds were almost out of ammo and rockets, and Bravo Troop with the APCs was under fire and out numbered. If that wasn't enough, I had Captain D at Battalion headquarters wanting a situation report. With the mortars knocked out and thirty or more of the Cong put out of action, the other two boats managed to get in and off-load the rest of the landing force and evacuate the wounded.

The Cobras from the 9th Aviation Battalion and six additional Hogs from Delta Troop arrived in the area about the same time. I advised the Cobras to cover the APCs from Bravo Troop under fire on the road, and the Hogs to my location. The bird I was in, as well as, the other Hogs we had arrived with were completely out of ammo and rockets. The Delta Troop Commander was leading the second flight, and took over my duties, and the original Hogs headed back to Battalion.

Back at Battalion, I was greeted on the tarmac by Captain D.

"What the hell did we run into out there?" I asked.

"Don't know yet, but it looks like a VC Battalion headquarters." "Pretty hairy out there huh?" Was Captain D's reply.

"Hell yeah." I said.

"Well better get back out there and assist Captain Chamberlin. I'll take *Backstop,* our APC's are in danger of being overrun." Captain D said as he headed to one of the Slicks loaded with additional troopers.

Our birds were already refueled and being rearmed now. With Captain D in the field my call sign changed from "Five Oscar" to "Five O Five" even though we would be in different locations, but on the same operation.

Soon we were ready and on our way back to the action. As we got close I called Captain Chamberlin to advise him we were back.

"War Wagon Six this is 505, over."

"Is that you Whitley?" The radio squawked back at me.

"In the flesh, with four *heavy*." I replied.

"Be advised, the Navy has two *fast movers* on the way, call sign Stallion. We're out of ammo, breaking off to rearm, out."

With that, Captain Chamberlin and his flight pulled out and we engaged. Two Navy birds arrived shortly after. I advised the MRF ground unit, who were holding their own, but still unable to move out, to mark their location with smoke, then called the *fast movers*.

"Stallion Lead this is 505, do you copy, over."

"Roger 505, this is Stallion Lead, five by five."

"Delivery from south to north. All east and north of the smoke is all yours, Roger?"

"505 this is Stallion Lead, I copy, south to north, target east and north of smoke, Roger?"

"Affirmative. We'll move to the river to get out of your way, out."

We and the other three Hogs took position above the gunboats along the river to watch the show. The two Navy jets made two passes laying their eggs, each time the shock waves from the blast rocked and swayed our birds, Warrant Officer Felton, one of the new pilots, almost lost control of his helicopter. The shock wave can catch you off guard the first time around. The jets then called and advised they were leaving the area. The jets broke the back of the enemy and allowed the MRF to move to the offensive, but it wasn't over yet. Another three or four minutes and a flight of four A1 Skyraiders arrived and lit up the Cong with napalm and rockets. They must have hit something important, because there were some hellish secondary explosions well to the north of us.

Captain D, also had the aid of a pair of Skyraiders and rapped up air operations with Bravo Troop. We rearmed and came back one more time, before concluding air operations along the river. What the ground troops had been up against was the Headquarters of the National Liberation Front's 311th People's Regiment consisting of approximately 350 soldiers, officers, NVA advisors, and political officers, as well as a Viet Cong training area and supply depot consisting of another sixty or so enemy. The battle continued on for another twenty minutes or so before the Viet Cong broke contact, picked up their wounded and disappeared into the jungle. The MRF had confirmed kills of 51 Viet Cong, and captured 12 wounded. Bravo Troop's numbers were 28 kills and no prisoners. On our side the numbers were vastly different. The Navy suffered 1 KIA and two wounded, the 60th Infantry, 2 KIA and five wounded, and Bravo Troop no one was killed and only two wounded.

Not all operations I was on were this intense, but they all had there scary moments that you don't think about at the time, because the adrenalin is pounding through your body. You actually get addicted to this rush after a while and miss it when you are in base camp or on R&R.

I don't think Mister Felton deserved the nickname he had acquired since joining the unit, which was Foul-up Felton, but if things were going to go wrong, he always seemed to be at the center of it. The day he arrived at Delta Troop he was two days overdue and Captain Chamberlin was about to list him as being AWOL. Felton said he had gotten on the wrong bird and ended up at one of Tan An's Fire Support Bases and had trouble getting a ride to Can Tho, even though the other three replacement pilots made it just fine. Then there was the time, I believe it was his second mission, he got into the wrong Huey and took off, only to realize it a minute later when the low fuel alarm started going off. His reputation was pretty bad with the Crew Chiefs too. He couldn't seem to keep one. As soon as replacements came in his Crew Chief would request a new bird and Felton would continually end up with the newest Crew Chief in the unit. Captain Chamberlin finally put a stop to that practice and started assigning more experienced Crew Chiefs to Felton's bird, but the more experienced guys were ending their tours and rotating out. So that really didn't help the situation. The guys just didn't want to fly with Foul-up Felton.

The big action came in spurts with the Cavalry. Oh, there was always something going on somewhere, but there were also times when the routine of daily life would take over. Time for drinking, time for playing poker and pinochle, and time for trips to Dong Tam to visit Madam FiFi's Steam Bath and Massage Parlor. My first trip to Madam FiFi's came when I was recuperating after being slightly wounded when our bird was riddled with small arms fire on one of the operations. As it turned out it was my last. I was wounded again a few days later during a poker game on one of the Navy boats collocated with us at Can Tho.

Before Madam FiFi's, during one of the lulls in the action while we were on a stand-down, and a lot of the guys were off on in-country R&Rs to Vung Tau or China Beach, the unit got tasked to deliver six new Hueys up country to An Khe. Of course I volunteered, it was something to do.

CHAPTER 21

The Lost Patrol

The day we were suppose to take the Hueys to An Khe, we got held up with one of those hurry up and wait deals. The new Chief of Staff for the 9th Infantry Division, Colonel Ira Hunt, was making his get acquainted trip to visit the Division units before taking his position on his ass at Division Headquarters. Basically he had an entire combat brigade sitting on their asses waiting for him to show up.

It was getting late when we finally got to Dong Tam to pick up the helicopters. I think we all figured we would spend the night and head out early the next day, but the Flight Operations Officer said the birds were ready to go and wanted us to leave right away. He said we could spend the night in An Khe and fly back tomorrow. Chief Donnie Wilson had flown the Slick from Can Tho that brought us to Dong Tam and I assumed he was going to fly it to An Khe, but I was wrong, I was going to be stuck with who else but, WO1 Felton. If I had known, I might not have volunteered, but here I am. As our bird was being refueled Chief Wilson, the other five pilots and six Crew Chiefs picked out the new Hueys they wanted to fly. Soon we were off into the twilight.

It was going to be a long flight. We were flying single file with Chief Wilson in the lead and Felton and I bringing up the rear. We were flying with plenty of spacing between the helicopters and minimal radio traffic, only the occasional, "How are you guys doing back there?" Our heading was 351 degrees. Felton was doing alright, even though he seemed a little nervous. It was simple enough, watch the altimeter, don't crash into the ground or the bird in front of us, and follow the strobe lights.

About an hour and forty minutes into the flight, it was darker than crap and we were starting to see flashes of heat lightning in front of us to the right.

"Ferry Lead to Ferry Flight. Wake up boys, we're about eight minutes out and it looks like we have a hell of a lightning storm to welcome us, and we're picking up some pretty good gust." Chief Wilson's voice came through the radio.

We were also picking up a lot of popping and cracking on our ground radio. It was intermittent and hard to make out, but it sounded like a ground unit trying to make contact. We really couldn't make out what they were saying so we ignored it at first. The closer we got to An Khe the stronger the radio call became, but it was still breaking up and intermittent.

"Ferry Lead this is Ferry Seven, over." Felton calling Chief Wilson.

"Don't tell me you're having problems back there Seven."

"No problems, but we are copying some broken traffic on 44.12 megs, sounds like a ground unit in trouble. Can you copy, over."

"That's negative Seven. The GRC radios are not in these birds yet. See if you can make contact, and I'll call An Khe."

I tried to make contact with the ground unit calling, but he must be having trouble with his radio. The signal was getting stronger but still broken. Even at that, he should still be able to hear us, unless his receiver is on the fritz too. The other six Hueys have landed by now.

"Seven this is Ferry Lead. Advise that An Khe is unable to copy anything on that freq. Better land that bird, over."

"Donnie, I can't let go of this. From what I can make out these guys are in real trouble."

"Damn it Felton, you land that bird. Understand, right fuckin' now." Chief Wilson was really getting pissed and I expected Felton to follow orders. The next thing I heard surprised the hell out of me, because I didn't think Felton had it in him.

"Ferry Lead, you are breaking up. Be advised, we are going to continue north for another ten clicks or so and try and make contact one more time. See you when we get back. Ferry Seven, out."

We continued on, northwest then northeast way beyond ten miles. We finally got a good strong signal somewhere north of Firebase Blackhawk. The transmission was still cutting in and out and about the only thing we copied was their call sign, Rover One Three and they were trying to make it to Blackhawk. We tried to make contact with them, but they just weren't receiving us. Finally fuel wouldn't permit us to stay any longer and we headed to An Khe.

When we landed at the airfield at An Khe, Chief Wilson was waiting for us.

"Get your asses over to the TOC, both of you, the S2 wants to debrief you." Chief Wilson was mad, but I think he was relieved to see us.

At the Tactical Operations Center we were interviewed by a Captain Firman.

"So tell me what you guys heard up there?" The Captain asked us.

Felton filled him in on where we first picked up the signal and where we followed it to.

"Is that it?"

"Other than it was definitely a ground unit in trouble with a radio that's only working intermittently." Felton told him.

"What about you Sergeant, anything to add?" Captain Firman asked.

"I think they said they were trying to make it to Firebase Blackhawk, but I'm not sure, and I believe their call sign was Rover One Three." I replied.

"Yeah, that checks out. One Three is a missing LRRP patrol. The last radio communications anyone has had with One Three was the Arty unit earlier today. Ok guys, thanks. We'll get on it at first light." "That'll be all."

The next day we all loaded on the Slick and flew back to Can Tho. Chief Wilson was at the controls.

———————

Two days earlier in the TOC at An Khe Specialist Roland Mack Clark and his Assistant LRRP Team Leader were being briefed on their next mission, even though they had only been back in base camp from their last patrol less than thirty six hours and should have been on a seventy two hour stand-down.

1200 hours day one - On a LOH, Light Observation Helicopter, Mack makes a quick visual reconnaissance of an area about twenty miles north of Firebase Blackhawk where other LRRP teams have been reporting suspected

NVA movement. Mack chooses his LZ and marks his artillery pre-plots down on his map in case a fire mission was needed.

1700 hours day two - On the tarmac waiting for the Huey that would insert them into Mack's chosen LZ. Mack rechecks all the equipment and goes over the operations plan one more time with the other three members of his team. Reconnaissance, ambush, and if possible bring back a prisoner are the mission objectives. Their helicopter is late and they don't get into the air until 1800 hours, twilight is approaching. Not a good start. It's not common practice to insert LRRP teams this late in the day.

1830 hours day two - As the helicopter approaches the LZ, Mack uses hand signals to insure the other team members are ready. everyone was good to go. The helicopter came to a hover above the ground. The bad thing about elephant grass is you don't really know how far you will have to drop, in this case it was only about 10 feet. The team exited the chopper and secured the areas until the chopper pulled out. Then the team quickly moved off the LZ towards the tree line, about 100 feet away with Mack walking point. elephant grass can be as sharp as a razor blade, so they didn't move as fast as they wanted to. On the way to the tree line, Mack noticed off to his left what appeared to be an open area with something that resembled a hooch. The closer they got the clearer the picture was, it turned out to be an observation platform with a roof looking out over the LZ. The team approached cautiously, but did not see anyone. When they got to the deck Mack saw a bowl of rice on the deck, at this time he figured the mission was compromised. Mack made radio contact and reported what they had found so far, when suddenly he was tapped on the shoulder and was told there was movement all around them. Mack stopped, listened and agreed. Mack called in a situation report and requested a fire mission.

1900 hours day two - It seemed like forever before the fire mission was approved. The team continued to have movement when the first round landed. Mack called in adjustments and the artillery battery continued dropping rounds, whenever there was a lull in the barrage of rounds, the team could still hear movement. Mack continued adjusting the artillery fire, dropping rounds closer and closer to their position as fragments began to come closer and closer towards them, Mack made the decision to make their way out of the area and had the two men without radios to drop their packs and booby trap them by pulling the pins on the white phosphorus grenades in their packs and to carry all the ammunition. Mack made radio contact with base camp and informed them as to what he planed to do. He maintained contact with the artillery and had them continue dropping rounds 50 meters to their rear to cover the escape route. Firebase Blackhawk was about 20 miles to the south and they began to run, with shrapnel coming dangerously close. Suddenly the artillery stopped and Mack realized the radio wasn't working and he could no longer make radio contact. The team continued running as far as they could toward Firebase Blackhawk.

2000 hours day two - Darkness upon them, they were still more than half way to the firebase. Mack decided to move off the trail and locate a good defensive position. With claymores set on their perimeter they maintained a 50/50 guard throughout the night. Mack continued throughout the night trying to establish radio contact, but never did. All and all the night was relatively quiet.

0600 hours day three - At day break Mack gathered the team together and explained to them that they would continue the march to Blackhawk. He tried to make radio contact again, but still no joy. As Mack was going to plot his position on his map prior to moving out, he had his weapon within arms length as he pulled out the compass and map to locate their position. Off to his left along the trail he heard movement, glanced that way quickly and saw three VC, there may have been more he didn't know, as he reached for his weapon the Viet Cong opened fire, rounds whizzed by and he felt something wet running down his left leg. Weapon in hand as he turned to return fire along with the other team members, a couple of grenades were tossed in the direction of the VC. The firefight didn't last more then five minutes. When Mack checked his self over he found a hole in his canteen and no blood on his leg. They then proceeded to check the trail and all they could find was a blood trail leading away from their position. Mack moved the team back to their defensive position, where once again he tried to plot their position. Just as he thought he had their position located, he heard someone over the radio. It was a Blackjack chopper pilot and he wanted to know where they were. In the clear Mack gave him their location, and within minutes they heard the helicopters. The pilot he was talking to on the radio told them to pop smoke so he could pinpoint the location. Mack popped white smoke, the pilot saw a purple one go off, so Mack popped another white smoke which the pilot saw and asked about their situation. Mack reported that they were recently in a firefight and expect some more company to come around. Mack heard the pilot radio in to base camp and informed him a reaction force was on its way.

0930 hours day three - When the reaction force arrived they followed the blood trail and ran across a bunker complex, tunnels, and killed seven VC.

1400 hours day four - A second reaction force was sent out and pulled Mack's team out for a debriefing at headquarters.

The Long Range Reconnaissance Patrols like Roland Mack Clark's team typically pulled these type of missions almost weekly their entire tours in Vietnam and were a vital source of first hand intelligence.

CHAPTER 22

The Final Days

I was eventually relieved of my duties with the 3d of the 5th Cavalry and finished my tour at 9th Infantry Division Headquarters in Bear Cat. I floated around headquarters in a couple of insignificant jobs waiting for my orders to rotate out of Vietnam.

Ten days to go and still no orders. I decided to make a personal trip to Personnel to find out what the hell is going on.

"Sergeant Whitley you should have had these orders two weeks ago." Said the Personnel Sergeant without apology.

"Well I didn't get them." "So when am I leaving and where the hell am I going?"

"Korea, in five days."

"Korea's ass Sergeant! I just spent a year and a half in Vietnam and three years in Europe before that. There is no way the Army can send me to Korea without my volunteering for it. In case you can't figure it out, I'm not volunteering, got it?"

"Sergeant Whitley, I can't do anything about the orders, they come from Department of the Army." The Sergeant said, and I realized it wasn't his fault and yelling at him wasn't going to change anything.

"OK Sergeant. Let's do this. I'm within 6 months of my ETS, end term of service, so give me one of those early outs that the Army is giving to the Draftees and I'll get out of the fuckin army." "How's that?"

"That's your choice Sergeant Whitley, but you'll have to see Major Brice, the Personnel Officer, first. I'll make an appointment for tomorrow at 1000 hours."

"Fine. I'll be here, with bells on!"

I called Colonel Augden at VE-AD to see if he could help me. I figured being almost on a first name basis with a full Colonel should be worth something. He wasn't there, but I did get to talk to Big M, and tell him my story.

Well, I met with Major Brice the next day. One of the first things he asked me was if I knew a Jack Roark at the Embassy. When I answered in the affirmative he explained that the Army was doing me a favor. If I went back to the States for assignment, I would be back in Vietnam in a year. However, if I signed an intent to reenlist and went to Korea for 13 months, I would be guaranteed a Stateside assignment at the end of my tour. He explained that the Army Policy had changed on back to back overseas assignments. Enlisted personnel could now be assigned three overseas tours in a row.

Major Brice said it would be a shame if I decided to get out of the Army, but if I was serious, I had two options available to me. ONE-Sign the paper work saying that I was not going to reenlist and he would change my orders to the Holding Detachment at Fort Dix, New Jersey for out-processing. However his recommendation would be number TWO. Take an intra-service transfer to the US Public Health Service.

"Doing what?" "I'm not a Medic or anything." I asked, and should have insisted on an answer. Oh well, hindsight is wonderful.

"Does it matter?" "They are looking for people with prior military service, at least two years of college, and best of all, the time you've put into the Army won't be wasted. It all counts toward your *twenty*. If that's not enough to convince you, consider that you'll make more money as a commissioned officer."

Well, like I said. Hindsight is wonderful.

I left the Army and after four months in school. I was commissioned as a Lieutenant in the US Public Health Service as a SCAT officer. SCAT stands for Supply Communications and Transport. In other words, if you're not a doctor, nurse, or medical technician, it's your job, no matter what it is.

I was assigned to the World Health Organization for duty at the WHO facility in Botswana, south central Africa. That is where I found out what my real job was going to be.

I received a briefing from a guy in a cheap seersucker suit, just like the one's Jack Roark is fond of wearing. His name was Sheehan and said he was from the American Consul, but I knew what he really was. He gave me an overview briefing on the Rhodesian war now under way. Including the fact that the United States had no involvement what-so-ever, including military advisors. So I was being assigned to a Rhodesian Home Guard unit as an observer from the World Health Organization.

Now a Home Guard unit is kind of like a civilian militia with uniforms and guns and very little training or supervision from the Army. Since reports of war atrocities have reached the international news, the Rhodesian government has agreed to allow observers from the International Red Cross and the World Health Organization to be placed with their military units.

Of course, my real job was to make intelligence reports to Sheehan and to report any special requests for equipment from the Commander of the unit, who was the only one who knew that I was really a contact to his *supporters* and a source of money when he needed it. Which was monthly. Some of his special equipment included Cuban cigars and a case of Pinch scotch whisky.

These are all stories for another time. After six months I was promoted to a full Lieutenant, that is the same thing as a Captain in the Army, so the pay was good especially since I was also drawing $20 a day in *per diem*.

I did the job I was paid for, for eighteen months then was ordered back to the States and was released from the Public Health Service.

I was out of the military a little less than a year when I got a warning notice from Department of the Army for recall back into the army. I decided not to wait for the recall and reenlisted, of course less than a year later I was back in Vietnam.

IN CONCLUSION

<u>COMBAT</u>. A man never knows how he will act the first time in combat. I believe it is truly out of his control. Hopefully his training will win out. That is why so much emphasis is put on training for the American fighting man. There are some guys that freeze and lock-up, the first time in combat. It is not cowardice. It is what I would call uncontrollable impulse. Most guys work through these times and revert to their training. The ones that don't, pay a heavy price in their minds. Luckily, I am like most of the other guys that served in Vietnam, things don't affect you at the time, but take their toll later. The problem with that is that they start to pile up on you after a while.

On Operation Norseman, in France, I was scared the whole damn time, but that wasn't combat. During TET on the berm, I wasn't scared at the time, and in

Cambodia and the Plain of Reeds, and on my time with a Phoenix K team, I had too much to worry about to be scared, but these times catch up to you later on. Even years after the war.

<u>CORDS AND VE-AD</u>. CORDS was the birth place of a lot of the secret missions during it's era, VE-AD was a way of implementing and paying for these missions and hiding the money from Congress. I tried to locate Colonel Augden and was unsuccessful, I'm not even sure now, that Augden was his real name.

John Falon Roark died in South America in 1984 in a plane crash, presumably, still working for the United States Government.

As far as the package I picked up at Fort Detrick for Roark, I have no first hand knowledge as to what it was used for. The Biological Warfare Research Laboratory, at Fort Detrick was closed in 1969.

After the fall of Saigon, Delbert Foo with his family moved to Hong Kong and worked for his father there. Cia and Alain Forette moved to France and operated a wine vineyard along the German border. Alain Forette died of old age in 1988, Cia passed away a year later.

<u>Chesterfield Three Zero</u>. Mike Brown was later assigned as an advisor to the West Virginia National Guard's Special Forces Unit.

On Valentine's Day, 14 May 1999, on what would have been Jeffrey L. Junkins' 55th birthday he was found dead in his home. Junkins died of an unexplained overdose of Veterans Administration prescribed painkillers.

The Nung soldier, that was bitten by the snake, made it to an Army Hospital in time, but died on a stretcher in the hallway, unattended waiting for treatment. He was not the only Nung soldier to be betrayed, or Montagnards tribesmen in general. We left them all behind when we pulled out of Vietnam.

The Chinese Pilot. I didn't use his real name because Official Air Force Records only indicate the pilot was rescued near the Cambodian border by Air Force personnel. There was no mention of him being purchased from a Cambodian Drug Lord, or the team that went in to get him. The hump we made into Cambodia was the hardest thing I have ever done in my life. It is believed by some Vietnam War Historians that China did provide some Mig pilots to North Vietnam, however, the man we rescued was one of ours.

<u>The road to Tan Tru and crash in the Delta</u>. Murphy the Crew chief survived Vietnam, took a medical discharge and lives in Huntsville, Alabama. Nyguen Tran Puk died in a Army Hospital after his burns became infected. Spec 4 David Feldman, the *Philly Flash* remembers the day different than I do. In his version he was the hero of the day, but I did find his letter very entertaining. Thanks, David.

<u>1st Air Cavalry Division</u>. Within four days of my leaving, the Air Cav recaptured the Special Forces camp at Lang Vei, and on every day of the operation the 1st Brigade units turned up caches of weapons and ammunition. One such cache contained 50,000 rounds of AK-47 ammo and 1600 mortar rounds. Operation Pegasus was terminated on April 14, 1968.

On April 19 1968, Operation Delaware was launched into the cloud-shrouded A Shau Valley, near the Laotian border thirty miles west of Hue. No allied forces had been in the valley since 1966, which was, at the time, being used as a way station on the supply route known as the Ho Chi Minh Trail. The first engagement was made by the 1st and 3rd Brigades. Under fire from mobile 37 mm cannons and heavy machine gun fire, they secured several landing zones. During the next month the brigades scoured the valley floor, clashing with enemy units and uncovering huge enemy caches of food, arms, ammunition, rockets, and Russian made tanks and bulldozers. By the time that Operation Delaware was ended on 17 May 1968, the favorite Viet Cong sanctuary had been thoroughly disrupted.

9th Infantry Division. The 9th Infantry ruled the Mekong Delta during it's time there. Many successful operations were conducted against the enemy. Within a year after TET 1968, the Division continued to decimate the Viet Cong and eliminated them from the Delta as an organized fighting force. The 9th Infantry Division, in conjunction with the Navy, introduced to the battlefield the Mobile Riverine Force, known as the MRF. This innovative unit took away the enemy's most valuable transportation routes, the rivers and canals. Although some infiltration of men and arms continued, they were insignificant in the overall scheme of things.

I will tell you flat out we were on our way to a complete military victory in Vietnam. The only war we didn't win was the one at home. Led by the anti-war demonstrators and Communist sympathizers like Jane Fonda.

The views I expressed in this book are mine, and whether you agree with them or not, I hope you enjoyed reading the book.